DON'T START NOW

TARA SEPTEMBER

Copyright © 2021 by Tara September

All rights reserved.

No part of this book may be reproduced in any form or by any electronic or mechanical means, including information storage and retrieval systems, without written permission from the author, except for the use of brief quotations in a book review.

Characters and events in this book are fictitious. Any similarity to real persons, living or dead, is coincidental and not intended by the author.

Editing by Anya Kagan of Touchstone Editing and Joyce Mochrie with One Last Look

Front cover by Cover Fresh Designs

PRAISE FOR DON'T START NOW

"I loved the push and pull between them and the feisty passion-fueled banter. It left my heart floating in the clouds and an unshakable smile on my face! Highly recommend!"

— *Red's Romance Reviews*

"A very enjoyable and entertaining read! I really liked the interaction and chemistry between Eve and Adam which kept me turning the pages until the very end!"

— *Goodreads Reviewer*

1

Only ten minutes past nine on Monday and Eve Richards was already wishing for Friday. Nothing like starting your workweek off with a ticket.

"You better hurry. The editorial meeting started," the latest college intern called from behind the welcome desk of the *Naples Tribune & Magazine*.

Overheated and out of breath, Eve checked the urge to snap at the poor girl as she raced through the lobby. *Why the hell do you think I'm sprinting?* She could damn well read a clock!

She passed her own desk without sparing the time to place her stuff down on the white IKEA workspace with dual monitors. Her editor in chief, Nik, already stood in the glass-encased conference room, examining the assignment charts projected on the wide, flat-screen panels. Every day he went through each staff reporter's workload in alphabetical order, assigning stories and checking on the status of previous pieces. Thankfully, he was only on Carl.

The smell of coffee wafted over Eve and she longed to pour herself a cup, but she was way too late for that. As inconspicuously as possible, she clutched the purse, which also doubled as her laptop bag, to her chest and slid open the large, sliding glass door. Spotting her at once, Nik arched a red eyebrow high over his rounded spectacles, continuing to address the group without pause, but Eve read the rebuke in his stare. Ducking her head, she tiptoed over to the only empty seat at the long, Formica conference table, right next to ... Adam Seager.

Great. As if her nerves weren't already shot this morning.

An intangible, electric current of heat seemed to radiate from his tall frame, only to slap right into Eve, causing her to stiffen. Ever the observer, the investigative hotshot silently scanned the room with eyes the color of coal, taking in all its details, occupants ... and her. His intense stares from across the office both delighted and unnerved her. She'd be flattered if she didn't know it was just his habit—the same skill that had made him famous. After all, his keen eye had led him to uncover Senator Jesse Clark's misappropriation of charitable funds and extramarital affair. Before that, Adam had served as an embedded journalist, bringing readers along on dangerous missions with a team of Special Forces in Afghanistan.

It was rumored he still had physical scars from the overseas incidents, not that Eve could confirm or deny that. Despite her own secret stares back at him, she'd never been able to spot any markings beneath his work attire. Whenever she pictured him out of his clothes ... well, scars weren't her focus.

Not that it mattered. She couldn't—and wouldn't—pursue a relationship with a coworker. Not again. So, despite the butterflies his rare smiles conjured up in her stomach, Eve did her best to ignore him. Unfortunately, he made that hard to do. For the last year, he seemed to enjoy going out of his way to rile and annoy her. Only her.

With a thrust of her hips, Eve scooted the large, leather chair closer to the boardroom table. As she slid, her bare arm accidentally brushed Adam's. She almost gasped at the intimate skin-on-skin contact. *Holy crap!*

The innocuous swipe felt as though a trail of warm, liquid chocolate had been sensually brushed up her skin, and damn if she didn't have an urge to lick it off. Biting down on her bottom lip, she noticed how his hand clenched his chair's plastic armrest.

Had he felt the heat, too, or was he annoyed that she'd accidentally touched him? She folded her hands together on the table, fighting the sudden need to brush against him once more to find out. "Sorry," she mumbled, trying to keep her voice low so as not to interrupt Nik, who was berating Carl for failing to get someone official on record.

Adam whispered back, "How's it going, speed racer?"

"What?" she asked, turning sharply to look at him, the faux-leather seat making a rubbery noise as she swayed. No one else seemed to hear it, but to her, each awkward squeak was deafening.

How could Adam possibly know about her minor run-in with the law? She grimaced just thinking about her morning ordeal. Eve blinked, remembering, and her heart thudded as red and blue lights strobed across the inside of her eyelids for a moment. If that sheriff hadn't nabbed her for doing a rolling stop, Eve wouldn't have been late at all. Seriously, who got pulled over for that? For Pete's sake, she was only making a right-hand turn onto an empty street. The same as every morning since she'd moved to the Southwest Florida gated community six months ago. Didn't the police department have bigger fish to fry? Apparently not.

"My contacts over at the precinct texted that O'Malley issued you a ticket this morning," Adam explained.

Eve opened her mouth in shock and again cursed herself at her stupidity for not doing a full, three-second stop. She hadn't planned on telling anyone about the humiliating experience, but of course Adam, of all people, had found out. Given his government and city beat, she shouldn't be surprised. He probably had plenty of buddies at the station. Not sure what to say, she pressed her lips firmly together. She searched his rugged profile, trying to gather her wits, but instead noticed again how his thick, black hair curled around the tips of his ears and the collar of his shirt.

He grinned. "I'm surprised you didn't bat those baby blues at him and talk your way out of it. Didn't know O'Malley had such resolve."

Snapping open her laptop, Eve refused to take his bait and get into yet another tête-à-tête with him, especially not in front of their chief. But Adam waited for her to respond, and dammit, she couldn't keep quiet. "I've never been pulled over before," she admitted in a whisper only he could hear. "I could barely find my registration and insurance card."

"Don't worry, speedy, I got you."

His teasing she was used to, but was he trying to reassure her? "You got me?" she asked, dumbfounded.

He nodded, bringing his elbows up on the table alongside her. She leaned closer to hear his next words. "Go ahead and contest the ticket. O'Malley won't show up in court, so it won't go on your record or ping your insurance. After all, he'll be too busy to appear, what with going to the Yankees–Red Sox spring training game at JetBlue Park. You owe me, though. I was really looking forward to that matchup."

What kind of bizzaro world was this? They were barely work friends. She would never have thought to ask for his help in this matter. Perhaps she was still asleep. Maybe she'd never gotten that traffic ticket to begin with and was still curled up in bed. She shot a nervous glance around the room, but no one seemed to be paying them any attention. "Are you serious?"

He quirked a brow. "About owing me? Damn serious. I had seats right behind home plate. But yes, consider the traffic violation dropped."

"Wow, thank you!" An ounce or two of Eve's morning stress released with her exhale, causing her posture to sag. The fine, combined with her insurance rates going up, would have blown her budget. She'd just saved up enough to fly to Atlanta to meet face-to-face with a prospective literary agent, too. Her travel guide plans wouldn't have to be pushed back after all. "Of course. I owe you big. Whatever you want, just name it," she rushed out in excited relief.

His stormy, gray eyes darkened before once again returning to their usual state of aloof amusement. With a lopsided grin, he bent closer to whisper in her ear. "Be careful, Evie, I mean to collect." His voice was a silky, hot caress. This time, she couldn't control the gasp that escaped her suddenly dry mouth.

"Eve!" Nik barked in annoyance, breaking her out of their increasingly intimate huddle. She jumped guiltily away from Adam. How many times had their boss called her name already?

"Um ... yes?" She met Nik's curious glare hesitantly.

"Glad you could join us," Nik said in his usual half-joking, half-serious tone. A few of her colleagues around the table snickered, sending a hot blush across her cheeks. "Your press trip next week on the seven-day cruise has been approved. I know I'm not supposed to say it, church and state and all, but the advertising department is particularly jazzed about this new partnership. Nice job bringing in such a big brand."

The heat in her cheeks only deepened at his rare doling out of praise. Well, hell. Her day was already an emotional whirlwind, and it was only nine thirty. She straightened in her chair. "Thank you. I'm excited, too." This was a career-making opportunity.

"There's just one thing," Nik said, shifting back and forth on the balls of his feet. "The higher-ups want this to be bigger than your usual travel stories. Possibly a whole insert with multiple articles, which is why we are sending Adam along with you."

"What?" Adam said sharply, rolling his chair forward as he sat up straight. "I don't do those kinds of pieces."

Well, excuse me! Eve dug her nails into her fisted palms.

"Exactly. That's why it's perfect," Nik replied. "Eve will be coming at it as a travel pro, and you'll bring both a fresh point of view and a male perspective. This way, it'll be relatable to all our readers, no matter how familiar they are with cruising. Sort of a 'he said, she said' piece from our very own Adam and Eve."

Laughter filled the room at the pairing of their names. Embarrassed, Eve cast her gaze down to her lap until their amusement died off.

"Someone down in advertising suggested that part," Nik continued. "However, it does have a memorable ring to it, so I allowed the digital team to mock up a logo and sidebar graphics for you two. I can see this becoming a regular feature, especially if your name is tied to it, Adam."

She could feel the blood draining from her face. This was supposed to be her big break, a chance to have her own byline appear on a travel piece and not with her ex or anyone else, for that matter. "But Nik," she sputtered. "The invite was just for me."

"Don't worry. We worked it out with the ship's public relations team and got an additional credential."

"Oooo, me!" Carl raised his hand and bounced up and down in his seat, as if on an invisible pogo stick. "If Adam doesn't want to do it, I volunteer."

"Put your hand down, Carl," Nik admonished. "This isn't the freakin' *Hunger Games*. You can't volunteer in his place. It's Adam and Eve or no one."

She glanced at Adam to find him already staring at her. Their eyes locked. His expression seemed unsure, almost concerned. How strange. Was Mr. Badass scared of doing a lifestyle piece? Sure, this wasn't his cup of tea, but it wasn't like they were being sent to a country on the brink of revolution. It was just a cruise around the Caribbean. Although, given his illustrious career, he probably would have preferred the former. Which brought Eve back to the question always on her mind when it came to Adam. Why was he here at the *Naples Trib*?

She wasn't alone, either. Everyone wondered why he'd taken such a huge step backward, trading in a high-powered career in Washington D.C. to cover a tourist destination and wealthy retirement town. He was older than Eve by possibly a decade, but that only put him in his late thirties, maybe early forties—hardly time to take it easy. It couldn't be writer's block, either, because he was still whipping up some beautiful, insightful prose, even if focused only on local politics.

"Now, Adam, before you go arguing about your responsibilities, if you ask me, a lighthearted piece once in a while would do you some good. As I've explained a thousand times, our readers do not give a shit about how many mayors are in the Cape Coral race this year. They would much rather learn where to take their grandkids on vacation, where to eat, or what new restaurant chain is coming to town. So, lighten up. You have this whole week to pack your bags and get things in order. Your itineraries are already on your desks." Nik jabbed his thumb toward the newsroom behind them. "You'll receive your boarding passes at the press check-in that day. Also, some popular travel publications are going to be on this trip, too, and management is excited that we're among the bigwigs for once, so play nice with them." Nik speared Adam with a look. "You understand?"

"Perfectly," Adam answered through gritted teeth and a forced smile.

Nik nodded and pushed his glasses farther up the bridge of his nose, a habit he displayed whenever he was uncomfortable. "Eve," he added, turning to her with a smirk. "Be sure and show Adam the ropes, introduce him to the right contacts and all that."

Adam snorted in obvious disgust.

She wanted to snort, too. *Show* him *the ropes?* Nik had to be kidding. The Pulitzer- award-winning Adam Seager taught a journalism course at the nearby Florida Gulf Coast University. She didn't need to tell him how to do his job. Then again, travel writing *was* a different beast than what he was used to. Eve couldn't picture him using all five senses to describe the tart and citrusy taste of a Mai Tai, or how it felt to spy a sunrise from the top of a barren Hawaiian volcano that resembled the red surface of Mars.

Hmm ... this is going to be interesting. So was going on a vacation of sorts with Adam. Definitely more than she'd bargained for when she first received the invite from Carousel Cruises.

Her normal, cheerful mood returned, along with her smile. Now why was her heart racing, just like when she was pulled over earlier?

2

As Adam walked back to his desk after the meeting, Bruce shoved his shoulder with a meaty paw. "You lucky bastard," the sports reporter said. The former college football player might have long since retired from the game, but he still maintained his athletic strength, despite the added padding. While Adam wasn't a lightweight, he still had to resist the urge to rub the impact area. "Eve to yourself for seven whole days on a boat?"

"Hardly to myself. It's a cattle drive. These cruise ships hold thousands of people. And you could hardly call it a 'boat.' Look at this thing." He waved the brochure Nik had left on his desk. "There is a climbing wall, a movie theater, and an ice rink."

"It's not the size of the boat that counts, it's the motion in the ocean," Bruce one-lined.

Good thing Adam had already eaten his lunch, or he would definitely have lost his appetite from seeing Bruce gyrate his hips to emphasize the corny joke. His belly drooped over his tight trousers and almost bumped Adam's desk with each word. Unexpected visits like these made Adam wish for his old, enclosed office space at *The Post*, instead of this modern, open-office plan. Fortunately, his work area was in the back corner of the newsroom, out of the way of any direct traffic, at least.

"Forget the ice rink, bro. I'm sure you'll be hitting the beach or the pool at some point, and she'll be in a bikini or some smoking-hot number, all wet," Bruce continued, giving him another nudge, this time forceful enough to propel the wheels on Adam's office chair into motion. Irritated, he had to uncross his legs and shove his feet down onto the tile floor in order to keep from rolling completely away from his desk. "Come on, she's girl-next-door cute, but with a movie star's figure." Bruce said, adding a creepy groan.

Humph. The jerk was right, and Adam hated him for noticing it, too.

Damn if Adam's imagination wasn't conjuring up images of Eve by the pool, too, leaving *him* feeling hot. As if his mind were an Etch A Sketch, Adam shook his head to clear his thoughts. "Keep your voice down," he admonished. "This isn't one of your locker room interviews. HR will have your ass."

"Speaking of asses, I want to have Eve's luscious—"

"I'm going to stop you right there," Adam said, holding up his hands, wishing he could shove whatever randy comment Bruce was about to say back into the man's bearded throat. He didn't talk this way among friends, never mind with a colleague at work. And he sure as hell didn't like Bruce even looking at Eve's body or commenting on any of her "luscious" parts. "This isn't a vacation. More like I'm going to be trapped with Little Miss Ray of Sunshine for seven whole days."

"Oh boo-hoo, cry me a river," Bruce said with a guffaw. "Speaking of temptation ..."

Adam twisted in his seat. Eve was crossing the room toward them, nodding and smiling brightly to everyone she passed. Her long, wavy, blonde locks swayed with her hips. The wedge heels she wore gave her a few extra inches, elongating her slender legs. Despite the added height, she was still a petite, perky package.

Now say that five times fast. He chuckled to himself, already in a better mood just from glimpsing her, despite the resulting gut twist, too. She never failed to do that to him. Counting to three, he blew out a fierce breath. She was walking happiness. Not in some phony way, either, because her smiles were genuine. She didn't fake it and had no problem holding her own or pushing back whenever he tried to poke holes in her flawlessly good moods. Hell, he loved provoking her until she revealed a different kind of smile, one reserved only for him.

"Hello, Bruce," she said with a casual wave as she stopped in front of them. And then in a more serious tone, "Adam."

"Richards," Adam said, mimicking her jaunty salute and professional tone when she addressed him.

There it is. My smile. He knew using her last name only, like some old newsroom crony, would do that.

"I was hoping we could discuss Sunday's trip," she stated, swiveling her gaze between them.

"Uh ... about that—"

"I'll let you guys pre-game," Bruce interrupted, already starting to trudge away. "Have a great time, you two. Don't do anything *I* wouldn't do," he added over his shoulder, loud enough for heads to turn.

Eve let out an awkward giggle before looking back up at

Adam, her forehead furrowed. "You're not going to back out, are you?" she asked, scrutinizing him.

"And let you go on a Caribbean cruise all by yourself? That can't be safe, and it sounds like you need a man ... to write with, that is."

Oh yeah, that was the look he'd been expecting. Why did he have to say that? He couldn't seem to help himself around her. He enjoyed pissing her off. Her sunshine face glowed even brighter when she was holding back her frustration.

"Oh, please." She released a sarcastic gust of laughter. "I don't need anyone, thank you very much."

"Okay, stop begging. I'll go. There's no need to say please and thank you."

"You're impossible. If Nik didn't just hint to me that our piece would likely get picked up for syndication from our sister publications, I'd ..." She trailed off and swatted her hand at the air. "It doesn't matter. We are teaming up, and I guess that's that. Did you have a chance to look over the itinerary?"

He was curious about what she was originally going to say but decided not to push her on it. He couldn't see the gain there as it wasn't likely positive, either.

"Yes, I just glanced at it. Ship tours, dinners with the captain, snorkeling, hiking, ATV rides on the beach, ziplining. Sounds like a packed schedule. So ... this is what you usually get to do on business trips?"

She stiffened, and he regretted the question immediately. "It's not as glamorous as it sounds. Well, it is, but it's not like I get to share those experiences with loved ones. Instead, it's usually with a mixed bag of journalists, strangers, and there's always a rotten apple or two in the group who spoil the fun by looking for negatives to exploit for clickbait headlines. And I'm always too busy trying to capture everything and remember what I'm feeling to even take it all in and enjoy the moment."

Sighing, she leaned her hip on his orderly desk, dragging his eyes like a guided missile in time to see her pencil skirt inch farther up her killer thighs. "You'll see,"—*oh he saw, all right*—"it's like going on a vacation, but seeing the whole thing through your phone instead of truly being there. I know, I know, woe is me." She released a self-deprecating chuckle that had his shoulders straightening. He didn't like his normally effervescent Eve sounding so cynical.

"I never thought of it that way. Your articles always contain such enthusiasm and wonder. I'm terrible at flowery descriptions, but you make it seem effortless."

Her blue eyes seemed to widen and soften with delight at his words. "I do? Thanks. Coming—that is, coming from you—that means a lot."

Note to self, praise her work more often and do not *picture her coming. Fuck!* It wasn't like he'd even have to lie in his praise, either. He admired everything about her, her prose included. Clearing his throat, he tried to break away from her smiling eyes, but it was a losing battle. "I just wonder … with such a 'perfect' schedule planned out for us, how can you tell what's real and what's just for show to the media? How can you know what the average Joe will experience if they go on the same trip?"

"Bingo. That's actually the most difficult part of a press trip. I just—"

He waited for her to continue, but she was gnawing on her bottom lip as if biting back the words she was about to say. Distracting, that.

"You what?" he asked, hoping she didn't notice the way his voice had cracked.

She released the grip her teeth had on her reddened lip. "I actually try to emulate you."

"Me?" he asked, dumbfounded, pointing a finger at his chest.

"Yes." She nodded. "The way you scan a crime scene or even a town hall meeting. Every room that you enter, for that matter. You calculate every minute detail. You can practically see the gears in your head whirling non-stop. So, like you, I try to look past what's right there in front of my face and take in the edges. I speak with the staff that's not assigned to catering to our every whim and ask how they like working there. I also rise early and walk the grounds alone and escape whenever I can just speak with tourists and hear how they're enjoying their trip. It's a combination of working with official spokespeople, experiencing the different activities they set up, but also finding my own sources."

"Boots on the ground," Adam murmured in understanding. He really did admire her work, her evocative descriptions, but now he was appreciating the skill behind her lifestyle pieces. She'd make a perfect guest speaker at his journalism class sometime. "When you put it like that, it doesn't sound different from trying to decipher the real meaning behind a polished politician's speech or a staffer's press release. Maybe Nik is onto something here with teaming us up."

He was surprised to see cheeks pinken, but he found it sexy as hell. Another thing he needed to do as often as possible—make her blush. Preferably from his kisses, but he'd take what he could get. For now.

"See, you'll be writing 'fluff' in no time," she said with a mischievous twinkle in her eyes.

He wasn't so sure. He was also irritated at how she kept putting down her beat. Recalling a remark he'd once said in an attempt to impress her, he wondered if he was partially to blame. Guilt jabbed him in the ribs. He was an ass for not rectifying her assumption sooner.

"This will undeniably be out of my wheelhouse. I've spent my whole career omitting opinions and emotions and just focusing on the five Ws. Yet, you also have to supply what you're feeling and provide advice." He groaned just thinking about it. He did not want to figure out vacation tips and sidebar pieces. On the other hand, this could be the new challenge he desired while saddled here.

She laughed, giving him an almost affectionate look. "For some reason, I thought you, of all people, would be good at giving your opinion."

He laughed, too. "Oh, really? What's that supposed to mean?"

"You know," she said, rolling her eyes. "You're so ... so forceful and confident, I'm sure it will apply to anything you write. You just have to open up and share a piece of yourself in the final work, that's all."

"That's *all*?" He gaped. "I'm definitely not comfortable opening up."

"I noticed," she said with a husky laugh that caused goose flesh to break out on his arms.

"Hey!" he growled, playfully nudging her leg with his.

"Relax, I got you," she said in a saucy tone as she echoed his words.

"You got me?" he repeated, an eyebrow cocking up in disbelief.

"I do," she said confidently, and patted his arm. "We'll work on it together."

He loved that she was caressing him, but a sisterly tap was not what he wanted from her. "We will?" he murmured, surprising them both by catching her hand and squeezing her fingers.

"Um ..." She looked down at their connected hands. "Well, I do *owe* you, right?"

"Eve." He drawled out her name slowly. "Exchanging writing tips and lessons on our craft is *not* what I had in mind."

3

What in the hell did he have in mind then?

Eve tugged her hand away, her lust-filled mind scrambling for something to say. Her heart hammered at the possibilities as she tried not to melt right off his metal desk and slink to a puddle at his feet. Likely, it was her imagination running a marathon. Adam was not interested in her that way, his odd behavior today notwithstanding. As always, she was reading too much into his intense, charcoal eyes. He'd discovered a new way to rile her was all. That must be it. He was messing with her.

And for the life of her, she couldn't remember his question. Oh, right. It wasn't a question. They were talking about how she could repay him. The tantalizing options flowing through her mind were not acceptable. She was sure she was blushing again from even considering some of the ideas that came to mind.

"I promise I'll pay you face value for those tickets you lost," she squeaked. Yes, she'd actually squeaked, and she almost smacked herself on the forehead for it.

Get a grip! He's been getting under your skin since you met him, and the moment he bats his long lashes that any woman would die to have, you turn into a blithering idiot.

His lush lips quirked into a lopsided grin that she'd come to know well whenever they talked. Staring at her intently, he shook his head. "I don't need the money."

"Then what do you need?" she threw back, her adrenaline rising like it often did when he baited her.

His grin turned downright devilish.

"Well, if it isn't Adam and Eve," Nik said from behind them, causing them both to jump slightly for the second time that day. The magical bubble around them popped. "Ready to take a bite out of the forbidden travel apple?" Nik asked, laughing at his own lame quip.

When neither of them answered, Nik shuffled awkwardly from foot to foot. "I'm having the intern arrange for a car to drive you to the other coast Sunday morning. Who wants to get picked up first?"

"Me," Adam answered immediately, and Eve threw him a curious look. "I'm ... uh ... on the way to Eve's place, so it makes sense."

"Oh? Where do you live?" Eve asked.

"In Naples," Adam said evasively.

"Yeah, I figured that, but where? How would you know that I'm on the way to Fort Lauderdale?"

"Because you live by the Interstate," Adam said matter-of-factly.

She placed her hands on her hips and tried again. "Yes, but how did you know that?"

"I'm an investigative reporter, Eve," he pointed out as if that explained everything. His nonchalance was becoming thoroughly irritating.

He was being purposefully vague. What was he hiding? For now, she'd let it go, but she wasn't going to leave it at that. She smiled inwardly, already drafting questions in her head to ask during their trip.

"It doesn't matter." Nik sounded impatient. "Whatever you guys decide, tell the intern, and she'll let the cab company know."

He walked away, leaving them both in a temporary silence.

"Is there even cell service or Internet on the boat?" Adam sounded concerned, but she was too focused on the muscles of his biceps outlined as he shoved his hand in his hair.

"Um," she said, clearing her suddenly dry throat. "Yes, there is Internet, but it's often spotty since we'll be way out in the ocean. It's just as well, though, since the Wi-Fi packages are often ridiculously expensive. I doubt Nik would approve the expense."

"No phones? How can we be reached?"

"Why? Who do you need to call?" She studied his concerned expression.

He didn't answer, instead asking, "What if there's an emergency?"

She shrugged. Was he deliberately trying to dampen her enthusiasm for the voyage? They'd been given a major travel piece, and this was a chance for her work to be read nationally. "I believe there's a ship-to-shore phone option, but I've never tried it." She snorted at his growing look of unease. "Personally, my favorite part about cruising is that you're forced to disconnect."

He grunted in answer, not looking pleased.

"I wouldn't have pegged you as a plugged-in guy addicted to his screen," she said.

"I'm not," he said tightly. "I just don't like the idea of going MIA."

She scrunched up her nose and paused for a second. Their conversation had grown tense, and she wasn't even sure why. She couldn't read his guarded expression and rigid stance. They needed to be talking about their assignment, though. Certainly not the time to probe into his communication fears.

"Let me know if you need a packing list or anything," she offered, hoping he'd take it as the olive branch she meant it to be.

He nodded, his body gradually relaxing, the familiar, playful smile tugging back at his lips. "I can tell you right now I'm not going to be wearing some Tommy Bahama luau shirt," Adam said, crossing his arms across the tight-ribbed, brown polo shirt that emphasized his pecks.

"Do you even own anything floral or tropical?" she asked, feeling at ease enough again to resume their lighthearted chitchat.

"Hell, no!"

Eve couldn't help but laugh at how horrified he sounded. "Well, I love resort wear, and I bet your midnight-black hair would look nice against some pastels for a change."

His dark eyebrows lifted. She shouldn't have gone into such detail. "Maybe something baby blue like your eyes?" he suggested, his voice as smooth as silk.

Again, with that? Who was this Adam doppelgänger? On a good day, she'd barely managed to spar with him or converse this long, but this flirty version of him? She could not handle it. "I ... I meant if you needed suggestions for packing things like sunblock, Dramamine, in case you get seasick, a waterproof case for your phone, stuff like that," she rushed out. "Oh, but now that you mentioned clothes, every sailing has a formal night, so don't forget to rent a tux."

"Evie, I lived out of a backpack for a year in the Middle East. I can handle packing for a five-star cruise. And I own my own monkey suit."

"Right." She gulped. He'd look better in a tux than any of the James Bond actors ever had. "Okay, then, you know where to find me if you have any questions."

Apparently, he even knew where she lived. Whether cowardice or self-preservation, something got her out of there before he could respond. Still, even as she walked away, she could feel his dark eyes on her like a beacon.

4

"It's weird, right?" Eve asked, plopping down on the purple, velvet settee in her friend and colleague's large corner office that overlooked busy U.S. Highway 41. Ignoring the seasonal traffic outside the tinted windows, Eve focused on a swaying palm tree branch instead. It had a calming effect on her. With an exhale, she released the tension from her talk with Adam before continuing. "It's like he doesn't want me to know where he lives."

"Yeah," Jada agreed with a slow, contemplative nod, walking over to the empty seat next to the couch. The red-bottomed soles of her high-heeled shoes flashed as she took a load off. While Eve yearned for designer shoes like Jada's, she couldn't afford it. And she rarely wore heels anyway, so what was the point? Besides, Jada wasn't a journalist on staff, but the vice president of sales and brand partnerships. She had an image to project.

"Maybe he's married with a family?" Jada asked, drawing Eve's gaze from her friend's shoes back up to her puzzled face. Married? The possibility had Eve's stomach turning, not that it should matter to her. "Noooo," Jada drew out, clearly thinking it over. "He's just a private guy, that's all. He's always struck me as a straight shooter."

"Yeah, you should have heard how he shot down working with me. Like the idea of us partnering disgusted him."

"Eve, come on, I'm sure that was due to the assignment itself, not about working with you. I think he likes you, actually. I've always thought so."

Jada was one of the smartest women Eve knew, so how could she be so off base now? "Definitely not," Eve said, crossing her legs and staring at the framed Spellman College diploma behind her friend.

Jada snorted and mockingly crossed her legs in a similar fashion. "He's always finding his way over to your desk."

"Our office isn't that big, Jada. And he never even speaks to me, except to torment me about something I wrote or to ask a work-related question."

Jada arched a dramatically penciled eyebrow, clearly saying, "My point exactly!"

"Besides, even if he did like me, which he doesn't, he's a journalist."

"Uh-huh, and so are you. It's perfect," Jada said, gleefully clapping her hands together like a wind-up toy with cymbals.

"It's the opposite of perfect. You know I'm never dating a writer again, and especially not someone I work with," Eve stated, adamantly shaking her head. "Mixing business with pleasure only works out in the movies. In real life, someone always gets screwed. And before your dirty mind says it, I don't mean screwed in the good way. Believe me, office romances are way more complicated than they appear to be. It's not just your heart on the line, but your career and reputation, too."

"At least our company doesn't prohibit workplace romances in our rules of conduct. And I'm confident you won't allow anyone to hold you back this time around. You've done a full one-eighty," Jada said, twirling her brightly manicured finger to emphasize her point. "Besides, not every man is like Hugh."

Images of her ex and their breakup flooded Eve's mind. Her feelings were still too raw to hear his name brought up so casually. No, Hugh and Adam weren't the same, but she'd learned her lesson about dipping her pen in company ink and then trying to write with it. *Fool me once, shame on me. Fool me twice, no way!*

"You don't think he's hot?" Jada prodded, taking a sip from her water bottle and looking as if she'd asked something innocuous, like the weather.

Was Adam hot? *God, yes!* Ruggedly so. Gruff in all the right ways. The kind of man who'd throw you down and ravish you. *Ravish? I've been reading way too many romances. Stupid, addictive Kindle Unlimited!*

Not to mention how the ground dropped away whenever he was near, or the ensuing electric current that ran from the tips of her toes to the ends of her hair. No, Eve couldn't deny that she was attracted to Adam, or Jada would flat-out call her a liar. She bit her tongue and decided to go with a dismissive shrug of her shoulders and hope for the best.

Jada sniffed at the air. "Do you smell that?"

"What?" Eve crinkled her nose and inhaled, trying to locate the source, but only saw her friend's satisfied smirk.

"It's strong, actually," Jada said, putting her hands on her hips. "It smells like ... like a load of shit."

"Okay, fine, and I'm knee-high in it," Eve admitted, and they erupted into laughter.

"We both know he's fine, so you better take every advantage of this trip—and I don't mean just your writing."

"It still doesn't change the fact that Adam and I work together, and that I'm never dating another writer again."

"Easy, girl. I'm just sayin', have some fun. You deserve it! I have a feeling you both do."

"Work is not fun," Eve said, standing. "Now, if you don't mind, I need to pack for my cruise."

Jada burst out laughing once again, and after a pause, so did Eve. "All right, I just heard what I said."

"Seriously, can we switch places?" Jada asked, still chuckling.

"Sure. I'd gladly have your beautiful life, married to Darius and mom to darling twins."

"Girl, I meant switch jobs, not lives," Jada said with a click of her tongue, but her smile was dreamy as she looked over at the family portrait on her desk. "Adam is great for you, but he's no Darius, thank you very much. Meanwhile, you're due at our place for a barbecue soon. The boys have been asking for you. Maybe once you get back?"

"I'd love to. Especially if you're making your mawmaw's yummy hummingbird cake."

"Now you're sounding like my husband," Jada said in a put-upon tone. Still, she nodded with another smile and returned back behind her desk to look at her computer.

Eve was lucky to have a good friend like Jada. After her breakup, she'd spent two weeks moping in Jada's guest room until she'd found a place of her own to lease. Luckily, it had been off-season in the resort town, or she would've had to tuck tail and head back home to Ohio where rent was more affordable. Granted, her new one-bedroom condo couldn't compare to Hugh's beach view high-rise that his grandmother left him, but it was hers alone and walking distance to a couple of restaurants. Not that she'd been going out much outside of work events.

Maybe Jada was right—she could use some lighthearted fun again. Still, a Mai Tai and the ocean should do the trick, not a roll in the hay. Especially not with a colleague. Even if said colleague was sexy as sin. No, getting involved with Adam would be career suicide and heartache city. She was sure of it.

5
―――

Never one to be late, or patient, for that matter, Eve stood at the bottom of the stairway to her second-floor condo on Sunday morning with her bags by her feet. She'd been packed and ready for days, and now she only had ten more minutes or so until the hired car would arrive ... with Adam Seager.

Glancing at her watch, she tapped her foot in anticipation. Not because of Adam, though. She was eager for the trip and their feature. That was all. It would be like any other work trip. It wasn't as if she was ever truly alone on these things, anyway. There would likely be a dozen other journalists with them the whole way. Except for their car ride over.

Eve scanned the quiet parking lot for the hundredth time, ignoring the couple in 1B who'd pulled back their curtains to watch her. They were harmless, but she could feel their stares and debated turning around to bust them. The approach of Ms. Maggie May from two doors over stopped her. The outgoing neighbor had introduced herself on the very first day Eve had moved in. She still wasn't certain if May was her middle or last name, but the older woman was a character, and it suited her.

"Going on a trip, dear?" Ms. Maggie May called out, her tabby cat, Bronco, trailing behind her on a thin, leopard-print leash, his fluffy tail swishing in agitation behind him. The feline clearly did not like their daily walks, but it didn't stop his cat mom from parading him up and down their street each day.

"Good morning," Eve returned with a friendly smile. "Yes, I'm going on a seven-day Carousel Cruise today."

"I love cruising," Maggie May cooed with delight. "Are you going with a fella?" she asked, waggling her eyebrows.

"No. Well, yes, but no, it's for work. I'm covering their new route and ship upgrades for the paper."

"Pity. My gal pals and I love a good booze cruise in the company of gigolos."

Eve's mouth fell open.

"Don't be so shocked. You're only as old as you feel, and from what I've noticed, I get out a lot more than you do, dear. Youth is wasted on the young. That's what I always say, isn't that right, Bronco?" As if on cue, the cat yowled.

"May I help you with your bags?" a familiar male voice asked from behind her, and Eve jumped, nearly tripping over her luggage. She pivoted on her sandals toward a white SUV that had pulled up while she was talking to Maggie. Adam stood there, motioning toward her things, and Eve nodded.

"Hello," she managed, sounding like the parrot in 2C.

"Hello," he said back, not at all parrot-like. Despite the fact that the paid driver had also come out to help, Adam rolled her suitcase to the open trunk and hoisted it in himself. Chivalrous, but Eve wouldn't have expected anything less from him.

"Now that's more like it," Maggie interrupted. "Have a great time, young man, and be sure to show her a good time. She needs it." The woman giggled, her cat meowed, and Eve darted inside the car before Maggie said anything else outrageous.

"Yes, ma'am," Adam said with a drawl and a pretend tip of a hat that he wasn't even wearing. "Younger sister?" he asked when he joined Eve in the back seat.

"Ha!" Eve scoffed. "An eccentric neighbor."

He bobbed his head, his silvery eyes full of laughter. "Nice place," Adam remarked, looking out the window and buckling his seat belt as they drove out of her palm tree-lined community.

"It's full of character," she admitted. "Most of the residents are retired or are here seasonally, so overall, it's pretty quiet and safe. I'm usually the only one at the clubhouse gym on the weekends or in the hot tub at night." His dark eyebrows arched ... because she liked to slip away to the hot tub in the evenings and look up at the stars? Seizing the opportunity to talk about housing, though, she smiled and asked, "Speaking of neighborhoods, how does this compare to where you live?"

His full lips twitched as he stared at her for a moment. "You have a hundred different smiles. Do you know that?"

His evasion was smooth, and her pulse raced under his unblinking, gray glance. "Sounds like you're avoiding my question." She placed her purse on the floor, wiggling into the plush, black-leather captain seat to get more comfortable.

"My place has even more retired folks." His grin was mocking and obviously intended to annoy.

Eve shrugged as if she were indifferent to the entire

conversation, but at least he didn't completely avoid her question this time.

"I'm serious though—I've never known anyone to have a whole library of smiles at their disposal."

She huffed out a breath, though his sweet comments were making her smile broader, which no doubt was his intention. "Yeah? And what smile is this?" she asked, turning in her seat to face him head-on.

"Ah, this one here," he said, pointing at her mouth, "is my favorite actually."

"Oh, really?" she said, trying to sound stern but failing to control her stretching lips. Maybe she liked the flirty side of Adam after all ... and being so close.

"Yes." He wagged a finger at her again. "This is the one that's usually for me. I'd like to think you're admiring my incorrigible ways and uncanny wit. Or, perhaps you're smiling like that because I'm just so damn handsome and you can't help yourself," he added, laughing.

She playfully swatted away his hand. "Dream on!"

"Oh, I will," he said with a shrug of his shoulders, drawing her gaze to the lightweight, pastel-blue polo shirt that he was wearing. She couldn't recall a time when he wasn't wearing dark colors or constricting business attire. He looked more relaxed, huggable even. Biting her lip, Eve tried her best to suppress the giddy delight stirring in her belly. Had he possibly selected the color for her, as she'd suggested the other day?

Focus! You have questions. Taking a deep breath to summon her fortitude, Eve opened her mouth to begin her first line of questioning, only to close it when he held up his hand. "I'm sorry, but I have to take a call," he said, looking apologetic. "I had an interview scheduled with the superintendent on Friday afternoon regarding the county's new zoning lines and school safety plans, but something came up and I had to reschedule."

"For now? On a Sunday morning?" she asked, not bothering to hide her disappointment. Was he deliberately trying to avoid talking with her? No, how could he have known she planned to use this ride to ferret out information on him? The corner of his lip twitched again, and damn if she didn't picture nipping at the seam.

"I'm on deadline and figured this was the best time. We have the next hour and a half free, after all, followed by a week of poor reception. Don't worry. I'll put my headphones on when I replay the live stream that they posted before my call."

So much for her interrogation. Adam pulled out his laptop and cell phone and was busy getting down to business. She needed to follow suit. What did it matter where Adam lived or who he lived with? She should be reviewing her questions for the cruise line and going over her research on each port destination. She was a professional, dammit. She better start behaving like one. With an audible *humph*, Eve slipped out her computer and placed it on her lap as well. Kicking off her sandals, she tucked her feet underneath her and tried to concentrate on the screen and not his profile.

Besides, she had seven days to gain further insight into the mysterious Adam Seager and still write one kick-ass piece.

6

Adam was duly impressed as he exited the gang plank and boarded the ship. Stopping short in the grand piazza, he took in the cathedral ceiling, a kaleidoscope of stained-glass colors and blown-glass shapes ornamenting it. From the corner of his eye, he could see glass-paneled elevators with golden railings zipping passengers up and down. He felt as if he'd just walked into a luxury mall, not a boat. Families and guests of all ages passed by him. It wasn't the cattle drive of seniors he'd been imagining. This was more like a floating palace.

He took a mental picture of the space and tried to memorize the feeling of awe he'd just experienced so he could describe it on paper. Wasn't that what Eve would do?

"Well, what do you think?" she asked, coming through the security checkpoint. She stood alongside him, readjusting her backpack and glancing around the great hall.

"It's not what I was expecting," he admitted, fidgeting with his askew credentials' lanyard that displayed his name, title, and publication. He tugged it off, untangled a knot, and then put it back on straight.

"It *is* pretty impressive. I think most people who haven't cruised before have all these stereotypes and preconceived notions built up in their heads, but once they step onto a real, quality cruise liner like this, they change their minds."

"Well, I admit, my mind is blown." He brought a fist up toward his temple and then opened it slowly to mimic his words. He was rewarded with another one of her smiles.

"You haven't seen anything yet. We'll have to go explore," she said with delight, tugging his arm for a quick second. "I'm excited to experience cruising through new eyes. The marketing group might be onto something here."

Adam followed her to the center of the atrium and tried to concentrate on what Eve was saying as she pointed out different highlights, but seeing her light up with enthusiasm and having it all directed at him was overwhelming. He stuffed his fists into the pockets of his trousers just to keep from pulling her into his arms to absorb some of her sweetness. Good God! He wanted to kiss her right there in the middle of the ship with tourists all around them.

Yup, he had it bad. He was beyond denying it any longer. Even though falling for a woman who would eventually be moving on to bigger and better publications, while he was forced to stay in Naples for the foreseeable future, wasn't the best of ideas. Falling? Ha! Too late for that. It didn't matter. He'd figure that stuff out later. First, he had to see if she even felt the same way. He knew what he had to do, too. He needed to open up and show her the out-of-office Adam and pray she didn't laugh in his face.

Operation Garden of Eden was a go, and he had seven days to make headway or return home a lonely failure. What did he have to lose? His aching heart was already in her lovely hands, which were now rifling through a folder of papers.

Adam bobbed his head, which Eve seemed to take as encouragement regarding whatever she was saying about the atrium café in the corner, but really, he'd been agreeing with himself to initiate full-on pursuit mode. He was prepared to pull out all the stops and call in favors if he had to. Hell, he'd already done that—and more—including going out and buying a dozen pastel shirts just because she'd suggested it, but he drew the line at busy, floral prints. Even the linen button-up he was in now he'd selected specifically because it matched the pale blue of her eyes. It was totally worth it, too, just to see how she'd smiled approvingly after spotting his new threads.

"What's your cabin number?" she asked, pulling him back to the present and right into her aqua eyes.

"Um ..." he trailed off, trying to recall his own name. "Caribe deck, room four-oh-four."

"Ha-ha, very funny," she said with a roll of her eyes, slapping him lightly on the shoulder with the folder she was still holding.

He stared, dumbfounded. What had he missed? "What's funny?"

"I don't know how you keep ferreting out this information, but you need to teach me your ways, Master Yoda."

"Huh?" He definitely wasn't following, nor had he pegged her for a *Star Wars* fangirl. He liked it, and being called master by Eve ... well, that was another fantasy entirely.

Eve crossed her arms over her chest. "Not only do you know what community I live in, you've somehow uncovered what room I'm staying in on the ship?"

Pulling his embarkation papers out from his laptop bag, Adam handed them to her. "I didn't uncover anything.

Look," he said, pointing to the document, "that's *my* cabin number."

"There has to be some mistake," Eve sputtered. Her alarmed expression was almost comical. "Let me double-check."

Eve fished through her own forms again only to reveal the same cabin number on her embarkation slip. She leaned forward to scrutinize the paperwork as if it would magically change, and he took the liberty of breathing in her bewitching, sweet-and-earthy scent—cherry blossom and almonds.

"Maybe we just have connecting rooms or something? Let's go see."

"Roger that," he said, already enjoying the trip and it had barely begun. She led him out of the atrium area and over to a carpeted staircase. Bypassing the queue for the elevators, they walked the three flights up instead. Their luggage was being delivered to their rooms—or rather, room—so he only had his go-to laptop bag slung over one shoulder. He offered to take her pack, too, but she refused, mumbling something under her breath that he couldn't make out as they climbed the stairs.

They headed to the starboard side of the ship and down the long, carpeted hallway until they found the cabin in question. Sure enough, both of their names were printed on the slip of paper next to the room number—Mr. Adam Seager and Mrs. Eve Richards. Given the salutations, someone in booking must have assumed they were a married couple. Whoever that inept person was, he or she deserved a raise. However the mishap came about, he was thankful.

Eve slid her keycard into the slot and pushed open the metal door. After all the horror stories he'd heard about small cabins, Adam was surprised to see such a large room. Two neatly made double beds with decorative pillows and plush bedding, an inviting, green couch facing a flat-screen television, along with a wooden desk, a mini fridge and wet bar, and finally, a wide balcony lay out before them.

Eve didn't look as impressed as she surveyed the room like a bloodhound. He tried not to laugh when she peeked her head into the closet cabinet, evidently hoping that it might lead to another room. No such luck for her.

"It *is* a suite big enough for a family of four," he commented, crossing his arms and continuing to watch her look about. "There's plenty of space for the two of us. There are even separate beds, too."

She set her backpack down on the desk with a bang and gave him an incredulous stare. "Yes, but we are *not* a family and ... and ... there is only one bathroom."

He shrugged, surprised she avoided mentioning the side-by-side beds. "We can take turns. Although, in an effort to save water, I hear it's best to shower with a friend." Somehow, he'd managed to deliver that joke without a smile.

She placed her hands on her hips and glared at him. He found it adorable. She was like a cute kitten trying to be a lion.

"All right, all right," he conceded with a laugh. "I was just trying to make the best of it and be a team player like Nik ordered me to be."

She continued her cat-eyed glare. "Since when do you follow Nik's orders?"

"When they suit me," he admitted.

She threw her hands up. "And *this* suits you?"

You suit me. Okay, he had to admit her fiery glower was starting to take on some heat. "Relax. We can ask the front desk if another cabin is available, and we'll get this straightened out."

"The purser's office," she corrected, and it took him a second to figure out what she was saying.

"Purser's," he repeated, slipping the agenda from his bag. "Whatever. It looks like our opening cocktail mixer is in less than an hour. I'll go see if I can find someone to sort this out while you get settled in."

Eve nodded, her shoulders visibly relaxing. "Thank you. I'll meet you there."

"Just in case, save me a drawer for my boxers, will you?" he called over his shoulder as he headed to the door. He weaved just in time, narrowly missing the frilly throw pillow she'd tossed at his head, which instead fell with a soft thud against the closing door.

He couldn't hold in his laughter as he headed back down the hallway to the stairwell. Yup, this assignment was off to a great start.

7

Adam spotted Eve's glorious tangle of blonde hair the second he entered the cabaret lounge. Granted, she would have been hard to miss, looking as bright and bubbly as the flute of champagne she was loosely holding between her fingertips and resting down by her hip. She was a vision, dressed in a gauzy-white sundress that clung to her breasts and then flowed in ribbons down to her tanned and toned legs. A mystical sea creature. A lovely mermaid.

The fanciful descriptions that were popping into his head had him chuckling under his breath. And he thought he couldn't write flowery language? The mere sight of her was turning him into a goddamned poet. Damned if he wasn't excited just being in the same room. She was bright, caring, and could twist his insides with a smile.

She was drawing more than just his attention, too. Not that Adam could blame the other men's admiring stares. Fortunately, her sight was glued to the porthole in front of her, which looked out over the Atlantic Ocean and the gradually departing coastline.

She tipped back her head, exposing a graceful neck,

while she daintily took a sip from the fluted glass. He was envious of the golden liquid invading her mouth. Just seeing her momentarily close her eyes to savor the sparkling wine before swallowing had him audibly groaning. It should be against the law for anyone to drink so sensually in public. It simply wasn't fair to mere mortals like him. Without tearing his gaze from her, Adam crossed the room.

"Look at this view," she said thoughtfully when he came to a stop next to her.

Staring only at her, he whispered, "I'm looking at the prettiest view right now." Yes, it was cliché, but he was only being honest. She was his favorite thing to look at. If she laughed in his face right now, he wouldn't fault her. He sounded like a pathetic pick-up artist. Still, he didn't expect the horrified expression that overtook her previously serene one as she turned to look at him.

No, *past* him.

"Oh no," she groaned, her face growing pale.

He reached out reflexively to steady her, afraid she was going to faint or be sick or something. "What's wrong?"

"What the hell is he doing on a cruise? He hates trips like this," she muttered, talking more to herself than to him.

"Who?"

"I'm sorry," she said, suddenly looking back at him in a panic and clutching his arm. "Ignore whatever is said, and please don't leave me."

"Never," he answered automatically, wishing he could fix whatever was bothering her.

"'Allo, there you are," a smooth, male, British voice said from behind him. "All right?"

Danger, iceberg straight ahead. Turning, Adam took in the slightly younger man, dressed in an overly nautical theme, including a blue blazer with shiny, gold buttons that had little anchors etched on them. Although they hadn't met, Adam instantly recognized the man's too-easy grin that didn't quite reach his eyes. He'd seen the insincere face often enough in the framed picture Eve used to have placed on her desk.

This was the other half of the long-distance relationship she used to reference whenever someone would ask her out, which was one of the many reasons why he never had. He didn't pursue another man's story *or* his girl. Adam Ethics 101. Six months ago, though, he'd delighted in seeing the photo of the two of them hiking at sunrise on some exotic mountain removed from its place of honor and tossed into the garbage bin. Out with the "rubbish," as an English bloke would say. Not that his nationality even mattered ... only his relationship status with Eve.

"You look brilliant. Stunning as always," the twerp said, embracing Eve and laying a kiss on her cheek.

Although irritated to see another man slide his arm around Eve's gorgeously bared shoulders, Adam couldn't argue when he desperately wanted to do the same thing. Apparently, her ex felt as if he still could. Adam straightened his shoulders, so much for his promise to Nik to play nice with the other reporters. Before he had the chance to brood further, Eve slipped out from beneath the man's possessive hold and his own posture instantly relaxed.

Her eyes narrowed. "Hello, Hugh. I'm surprised to see you on a commercial trip like this." Her perpetually upbeat voice was cool and monotone, her walls building up.

"Yes, well, normally I wouldn't dream of it, but then I heard you were going and I thought I'd surprise you. So, I decided to simply show up," Hugh said, all puppy dog-eyed. "Surprise!"

Oh, fuck no. This was *his* chance with Eve. Adam didn't

need some refined douche getting in the way. The man had his chance and apparently blew it. Adam loudly cleared his throat, causing the guy to finally take in his presence. Hugh's icy-blue gaze darted from Eve's face to Adam's for only a brief moment, but long enough to convey his annoyance.

"Sorry," Eve chimed in, visibly shaking herself out of her stupor. "Hugh, I'd like you to meet my *friend* and colleague, Pulitzer-Prize winner, Adam Seager."

The way she'd emphasized the word friend with extra feeling, combined with her award dropping, had Adam arching an eyebrow. Since when did she give a crap about his Pulitzer? Unlike the rest of their colleagues, she'd never even asked him about it or his past exploits. More than once, he'd caught her rolling her eyes when people referenced his career achievements. He didn't care about the awards, either, but oddly, he did care that she didn't.

"Adam," Eve continued sweetly, resting her delicate hand on his shoulder as if she'd made the intimate gesture a hundred times before. A feeling of contentment washed over him. "This is Hugh with *Elite Traveler*."

"You failed to add award-winning before my name, too, love," Hugh remarked while reaching out to grab a cocktail from a passing server, seeming not the least bit impressed with her introduction. "I might not have a Pulitzer, but I do have several bestsellers, one of which is in the gift shop on board, and I can't even count how many times *Nat Geo* named *me* Best Travel Writer. But who's counting, right?" Hugh gushed with a smirk.

Apparently, Adam had just been entered into a pissing contest. Hugh continued to smile, roaming his ice-blue eyes covetously over Eve's slender figure and lush curves. Eyes that Adam unreasonably wanted to blacken. Finally, Hugh turned his pretty-boy face back toward Adam again. "How do you do?" he asked with as much interest as a bored teenager.

Neither of them bothered to raise a hand for a customary shake. "Fine. How do *Hugh* do?" he shot back in return, giving the pansy his best back-off glare.

"Cheeky," Hugh clipped out, nodding regally as if conceding an imaginary point. Turning a cool smile toward Eve, he added, "I thought you'd be happy to see me. I'm making a grand gesture here," Hugh said, spreading his arms wide and shaking his head, but his standard, Oxford haircut barely moved. "Can't you see I've missed you like mad? You won't return my calls or messages. You've left me no choice. I'm only here on this horrid commercial liner so I can see you. To make amends. To grovel at your feet. Whatever it takes."

Godammit! Adam felt like roaring like a wounded beast upon hearing her ex's confession.

"Seriously?" Eve said, downing her champagne in one swift motion. "Nothing has changed, Hugh. You know why I left."

Hugh stepped forward, and Adam's eyes darted between the pair as if watching a tennis match.

"We were friends first, weren't we?" Hugh asked entreatingly. "We've known each other far too long to let it end like this. Besides, we have seven fun-filled days ahead of us."

"They no longer sound so fun," Eve said flatly, slamming her glass down on the high top next to them.

Ditto to that! Adam took a purposeful step closer to her, looming over Hugh in the process. Once again trying and failing to get the bastard's eyes on him instead of Eve's cleavage.

"Please," Hugh pleaded, looking solely at Eve. "Let's

head up to my cabin and talk this whole thing out. I can make it up to you. I promise."

Adam silently willed Eve to say no. He didn't want to have to confess his own feelings in front of this prig. Both of them begging before her. His chances were deteriorating by the moment, and given the history the two apparently had, Adam didn't like his odds.

And what do Eve and I even have? A working relationship, witty, back-and-forth stolen glances, innocent touches full of heat? Definitely not an equal battlefield.

"It's too late. I've so moved on, it's scary," Eve finally said as if quoting a memorized lyric, her voice wavering slightly. "Besides, Adam and I were just about to escape back to *our* cabin for some alone time before the next required meetup."

"You're sharing a room?" Hugh yelped, putting his hands on his hips and bristling like an agitated peacock. "With him?"

The way he'd said *him*, Hugh might as well have been referring to a flea-infested mutt. Fisting his hands, he checked the impulse to growl back like an angry dog.

"Yes," Eve said, linking her arm with Adam's and drawing her tempting curves up alongside him, suddenly clinging to him like a contented kitten. "Isn't that right?" she practically purred.

Adam couldn't contain his grin. She'd chosen him, even if it was only a farce. Dropping his arm around her slender waist, he pulled her even closer against his chest.

"*Hugh* betcha, dumpling," he teased, holding in the *oomph* her elbow jab to his side caused. He'd never called a woman that ridiculous pet name before, but he knew it would rile her and hopefully bring her thoughts away from Hugh. It was worth her pathetic punishment. In a more serious tone, he murmured, "I can't wait to ditch this mandatory event and have you all to myself."

Truer words were never spoken. She felt great in his arms, fitting perfectly under his shoulder. Belatedly, he realized, he was only punishing himself, having her pressed so tightly to him. With each heave of her breath, her breasts moved against him. *Damn.*

He loosened his hold. Looking down and getting lost in her wide, pleading eyes, he almost forgot that Hugh was standing there until the man cleared his throat, interrupting their silent communication.

"Hmm?" Eve moaned vaguely, not breaking their shared stare.

Adam smiled at the obvious slight.

"I ... I said, I'll see you at dinner later," Hugh snapped, every line of him vibrating with hostility.

Before Eve could reply, Adam responded drolly, "*We* will see you at dinner. Drinks are on me."

Hugh scoffed. "It's a *hosted* dinner. Drinks are already included."

Adam grinned wider, enjoying being able to ruffle the man's peacock feathers so easily.

Eve chuckled, her body moving deliciously against his in the process once again. "He knows that, Hugh, he was being funny."

He swelled with pride that she understood his humor.

"I hope he didn't win the Pulitzer for comedy writing," Hugh groused, pivoting gracefully on his tan loafers and leaving with a curt nod. Adam almost felt bad for the pompous jerk, but only for a millisecond. Besides, it was hard for him to feel anything but Eve in his arms at the moment.

Once Hugh disappeared from view, she sighed and

sagged against him. "Thank you," she said, craning her neck back to peer up at him with a sweet smile. He immediately wanted to kiss her to see if she tasted as sweet. She likely would.

Unable to speak just yet, he nodded stiffly, still not letting her go. She didn't seem to be in a rush to separate, either.

"Ex-boyfriend?" he finally asked, already knowing the answer but hoping to prompt her for more details, a skill he'd honed over the course of his career of asking questions.

"Ex-fiancé," she corrected, unknowingly kneeing him in the balls with her admission. "We met years ago on a month-long writing fellowship throughout India, and ... well, we were the only two reporters who spoke English."

His gaze jumped to hers as frustration raced through him. "And that's all it took?"

"No, of course not. I was young and impressionable, and his writing prowess and experience actually intimidated me in the beginning. Kind of like when I first met you."

He abruptly let her go so he could get a better look at her face. "I intimidated you?"

"God, yes," she admitted, smoothing down her rumpled dress and not meeting his gaze. "You still do."

"I never meant to," he answered honestly.

"Come on, you love teasing me," she huffed, rolling her eyes as he stood silent. "And you know you drive me crazy."

Yes, he wanted to tease and drive her crazy, but not in the way she meant it. Hell, if anyone was driving anyone crazy, it was her tempting body and bright personality tormenting him on a daily basis for the last two years.

"I never would have guessed that, considering how you always give it right back to me. Shutting me up like no one else can."

"I can?" she asked skeptically.

He smirked and mimicked the motion of zipping his lips shut. She laughed, just as he hoped she would.

"Anyway, thank you for playing along with me and the whole shared cabin excuse," she said, sagging against him once more.

Her use of the word *playing* removed his smile. He wasn't playing. He wished he had a right to hold her close like this. Just knowing that Hugh, at one time, must have had that privilege was pissing him the hell off right now. No, when it came to Eve, he was only "playing" for keeps. Even if that meant people commenting on the fact that they were Adam and Eve for the rest of their lives. She was worth it. Hell, his parents were Spencer and Tracy. If they could do it, so could he.

"He was the last person I was expecting to see, and I guess I panicked. Hopefully, though, your presence will keep him from attempting to get me alone again."

"Are you afraid to be alone with him?"

"No, it's not that. I just don't want to rehash it all again. There's no point. I've said my piece, and it's not like he can change the past."

Adam tried to keep himself from prying—really, he did—but he couldn't help it. The journalist in him wanted to pepper her with a thousand questions, and the man who desperately wanted her needed to know more, especially if she still had feelings for Hugh. "Did that bastard cheat on you?"

"He didn't cheat *on* me," she said with an unhappy laugh, "but he did cheat me."

"Excuse me?"

She sighed. "That last book he wrote, his latest bestseller ... well, I helped him write it. We spent a year working on it.

It was my first time attempting to write long form, and it was grueling. Even when Hugh was traveling solo, I spent almost every night writing and editing his drafts, which is why I always missed out on our post-work happy hours. Anyway, I was supposed to receive a co-author credit, but he said his publisher wouldn't allow it, so he had no choice but to drop my name before going to print. It hurt, but I stupidly stood by him, assuming he'd include me in the acknowledgements or in the dedication. In the end, he didn't even have the decency to include me in his acceptance speech. He thanked his prep school history teacher and not me."

"Are you telling me," he said slowly, "that he chose a stupid book over *you*?"

"I suppose so," she said with a weak shrug.

To hell with it. He gathered her close and hugged her tight. "What an ass. I'm sorry."

"Ancient history," she said, but the pain on her pale face told a different story. Abruptly, she froze in his embrace. "Oh my god, this is going to backfire on me. If Hugh finds out that I lied and made up a fake relationship between us, he'll rightfully assume I'm not over him and double his efforts."

"Then we can't let him find out," Adam agreed.

Staring off toward where Hugh had exited, Eve nodded her agreement. "If you don't mind, maybe we can bunk together after all?" She turned to him, big eyes pleading. "Like you said, it *is* a suite. We can make it work."

Aw shucks, twist my arm, why don't you? He had to curl his toes in order to plant himself firmly to the ground just to keep from excitedly twirling her right there in the lounge. The crew at the purser's desk had already informed him there wasn't a free cabin available, but she didn't need to know that.

"No problem. I'll gladly be your bodyguard on this

trip." *I would love to guard every inch of your body. Especially from Hugh.* "Just say the word, and I'll throw him overboard."

"That won't be necessary," she said with a laugh, the color returning back to her cheeks. "But please, feel free to continue to remind me that he's an ass and keep me away from temptation, okay?"

"Oh sweetie," he answered with a throaty chuckle and shake of his head. "I can't promise you that. I plan on tempting you every chance I get this trip."

Rolling her eyes, she swatted him lightly, as if he was kidding. "I really do appreciate it," she said more seriously.

"You know with this extra favor ... this means you're going to have to owe me yet again. You're really piling up your debt, Richards."

"I see you're counting." Her blue eyes held a glint of amusement. "And you plan on collecting, right?"

"Most definitely," he said unequivocally.

"But how can I make it up to you? What could I possibly have that you'd want?"

His words stuck in his throat. Was she fucking with him? He searched her face to see if she was flirting or being coy, but she looked dead serious. Well, fuck, what woman would ask a naïve and loaded question like that? Didn't she realize how attractive and temptingly sweet she was? That any man in his right mind would take advantage of an open-ended suggestion like that?

He was already tilting his head down to meet hers in answer when the ship's warning system blasted out three steady whistles, effectively cooling his jets and saving him from pressing his luck too soon.

A pre-recorded message played over the loudspeaker, indicating that this was "a drill, and only a drill" and that everyone should report to their muster station for a mandatory safety exercise.

Before either could speak, the room's occupants swarmed the exit, effectively separating them as everyone herded out to their designated areas.

8

When had she boarded the ship of fools? She certainly felt like one, lying to her ex and forcing her colleague to go along for the ride. As if they were all trapped in some Hallmark TV movie. But it was the first thing that popped into her mind with Adam's strong and steady presence next to her. She'd practically flung him in front of her like a shield. Of all the places, she never thought she'd see Hugh here. She had never wanted to see him again, never mind be on a trip with him like they used to. This was supposed to be her chance back at serious travel writing without him. Without anyone, for that matter.

You could call it fate, but then, Hugh admitted he was only on this trip because he'd found out she was attending. What was it lately with everyone knowing more about her life than she did?

She stole a quick glance at Adam, seated next to her at the large, round table in the ornate dining room with a Parisian theme. Hiding behind the leather-bound menu, she felt like an inept gumshoe. Fortunately, he didn't seem to notice her lack of stealth as he was speaking to the woman on his left, an editor with a travel agency publication. Patrice? No, Pamela!

About a dozen fellow reporters occupied the other seats, along with several more at an adjacent table to them. Hugh hadn't arrived yet, which was no surprise. He detested organized trips and following a program that he didn't devise himself. He'd likely skip out on many of the planned activities on their itinerary, much to the annoyance of the haggard organizers. Except, here he was, entering the dining hall, purposefully striding toward her. He tipped his head when their eyes met. His hair flicking back expertly, a movement that used to make her sigh. Now she fought the urge to gag at the practiced move.

Still speaking to Pamela about the craft beer options on the ship, Adam draped his arm on the upper back of Eve's chair, slightly grazing her loose hair in the process. The faint touch sent awareness shooting through her, and it had nothing to do with her ex-fiancé's approach.

Hugh's eyes narrowed to slits, focusing on Adam's casual lean. Thankfully, their trip coordinator, Natalie, placed Hugh across from the two of them instead of at the open seat on Eve's right. She sighed into her wine goblet with relief. If he wanted to speak on a personal level, he'd have to do it across the dining room table. Given how easily embarrassed Hugh was by anything as unconventional as that, he would keep things professional, for the time being at least. He still managed a scowl at the haggard coordinator, whose smile faltered as she stepped back to check on her other guests.

The maître d' provided introductions to the staff, along with his meal recommendations and inspirations behind the various French dishes. In an effort to appear like a doting couple, Eve suggested Adam and she go surf and turf with promises to share each other's plates. She only hoped he wasn't planning on feeding her from his fork, too, but given Adam's sense of humor, she was already laughing to herself at the juvenile image it presented. She doubted he'd miss an opportunity like that to make her uncomfortable.

Of course, Hugh thought sharing a dish was disgusting. He'd once called her a scavenger for eating off his discarded plate, but that pork belly had been too scrumptious to leave behind. Was he recalling that time, too, as he watched her and Adam order in harmony?

After their appetizer plates were collected, the white-uniformed waiter placed a sorbet at everyone's place settings to cleanse the palate before the main course came out. It seemed to loosen Hugh's tongue as well. That and likely the glass of red wine he'd downed. "And how many times have you sailed, Adam?" Hugh asked, attempting conversation across the divide.

"Wouldn't *Hugh* know it?" Adam replied affably, pushing aside his empty glass bowl. "This is my first time, Hugh."

Hugh gritted his teeth. "Surely, you mean this is your first time on this common cruise line," he prodded.

"Nope, my first time on any cruise liner," Adam corrected. Leaning in Eve's direction, he murmured for her ears only, "And don't call me Shirley." She snorted, finding it difficult to swallow the sorbet she'd just put in her mouth. Hugh's face turned red.

"How refreshing," Hugh mocked, but Adam simply shrugged one shoulder in indifference.

"Adam might be new to cruising, but he's spent time overseas in the Middle East as a war correspondent," Eve chimed in.

"How sweet. She even speaks for you," Hugh said, indicating with a nod to the waiter that he'd like a new glass of Beaujolais poured for him.

"Isn't it?" Adam said, making it sound more like a statement than a question. "I'm damn lucky to have someone as strong and smart as Eve in my corner. And *I'm* smart enough to never let a woman like that go. Too bad you can't say the same, Hubert."

She gasped, choking again on her gelato. Reaching for her water, she tried to keep from coughing all over the table. Adam patted her back as she regained her composure. Even after she was in control again, he let his hand linger, leaving a trail of heat in its wake.

Hugh's lips were pressed together so tightly, the color drained from them, making them a shade lighter.

"Which port is everyone most looking forward to?" Natalie interrupted, the rebuke in her tone obvious.

The group eagerly called out their responses.

"Punta Cana."

"Aruba."

"Belize."

Adam smiled, lifted his glass to his lips, and left Natalie's question unanswered. Leaning closer to Eve's ear, he stage-whispered, "Our cabin." A shiver ran through her from the heady combination of his nearness, the tickle from his breath, and his use of *our*. She could feel herself blushing. Still, she probably was not as red-faced as Hugh after overhearing Adam's not-so-subtle comment.

She should feel guilty for enjoying Hugh being tormented, but thoughts of him altogether flew from her mind when Adam brushed her shoulder as he reached for his glass, a whisper-light touch that made her breath catch. A tremor trickled through her. The chills this man could cause were evidently numerous. She swiveled her gaze from

Hugh's narrowed stare up into Adam's dark eyes, which were somehow sensually darker. She felt herself drawing closer, as if he were the only lifeboat left at sea. His heated look pulling her to him. She needed to swim away pronto.

As if reading her mind, his full lips twitched and he leaned in. "Pucker up, buttercup," he muttered so only she could hear. He spoke with confidence, his dark gray eyes smoky with pleasure.

"What? Here?" What had gotten into him?

His mouth broke out into a sexy smirk. "Aren't we supposed to be putting on a show?"

"We're still professionals on this trip. We don't have to kiss in front of everyone."

The gleam in his eyes reflected his amusement. "Against a little PDA?"

"No, yes," she sputtered, adding, "Hugh always was."

"Perfect, let's show him how it's done. Come on, he's watching."

She shot a quick glance across the table before she leaned up to give Adam the quickest of pecks. However fleeting the contact, the resulting warmth lingered on her lips.

"You can do better than that. I'm not your brother," he teased.

"I don't have a brother," she replied matter-of-factly, then realizing what she said, she sucked in her breath. "Not that I'd be kissing him if I did."

Adam laughed quietly and resumed his gradual movement forward, and God help her, she couldn't wait. The pull was irresistible, which left her heart racing in fear.

"Bon appétit!" the head waiter declared, reaching between them to place their dishes on the table, effectively clipping the invisible string that was pulling her under.

Gulping, Eve straightened and pushed her wine glass farther away. She needed a clearer head if she was to sit this close to Adam and not look like an unprofessional idiot. "Oh good," she declared, brighter than she was feeling. "I'm hungry."

"Me, too," Adam agreed in her ear, his voice a husky caress. That did it. Under the table, she nudged his knee with hers. He had the nerve to chuckle. Sexily, at that. She couldn't take much more of this. If it weren't a strip steak in front of her, she probably wouldn't have been able to eat a bite, her nerves were so wrecked. But like Adam, she found the meal hard to resist. She barely had the presence of mind to remember to leave behind a piece for her faux date to share.

Watching Adam savor each bite made her mouth dry. Of course, he had to like a rare steak, too. *Ugh!* He'd also left her a bigger portion of his meal than she had for him. *Oops!*

When their dessert plates were collected, Eve declined an after-dinner drink, eager to excuse herself and collect her muddled thoughts in her cabin—a cabin she shared with Adam. Her heart thudded faster and she turned to look at Adam, only to find he was already watching her, his eyes hooded. *Gulp.*

"Shall we?" he asked, rising to pull out her chair as she stood on wobbly legs. Was it her imagination, or was there a sudden lack of oxygen in the room?

"Come now, you two. You're not seriously going to call it a night already, are you?" Hugh asked, his voice hitching. "Not very adventurous or sporting to this wonderful group, especially as we're just getting to know one another and this magnificent ship. What do you say we all head to Bon Voyage Karaoke in the night club?" He sent the table a dazing smile, along with a wink at Natalie.

The woman eagerly jumped aboard the invitation, her head bobbing almost as fast as she talked. "Oh yes, that would be perfect. The adults-only space was recently renovated, and they will be doing sign-ups tonight for Ship Idol, which is always a must-see competition on every sailing."

The group mumbled in agreement as they rose to their feet. So much for giving her nerves a break. Then again, Hugh's stunt bought her time before having to be alone with Adam in their shared cabin so soon. Her gut twisted with excitement and uncertainty. Rising from her seat, Eve collected her things and marched on.

9

You've got to be fucking kidding me!

Of course, the wanker could sing, too. Adam was no Simon Cowell, but even he recognized Sir Phony had talent. Hugh knew it, too, relishing the attention as he worked the room.

Whatever. Adam took a swig of his beer directly from the bottle, because really, what else could he do but sit there and watch the man showboat?

"You say the world has come between us, our lives have come between us...."

Stepping down from the stage with the cordless microphone still in his hand, Hugh danced forward, not missing a lyric despite no longer being able to see the screen that provided the words. His destination was clear—Eve.

She sat up straighter in the barstool and inhaled deeply as Hugh approached their table.

"I see you, the only one who knew me, but now your eyes see through me...."

She vehemently shook her head at him. Hugh nodded

back as he continued to sing and glide toward her, his gaze focused on only her.

"Come on, Eve, join me!" he said over the microphone, and as if on cue, the crowd roared to life at his request. He held out the mic in front of a stunned Eve.

"And I said, what about Breakfast at Tiffany's? She said ..."

After a prolonged second, Eve released the tension in her shoulders and leaned forward. She reached up to take Hugh's extended hand, joining him out on the dance floor as she sang the next couple lines. Hugh sang back into the mic, their heads close.

"And I said, well that's the one thing we've got."

Eve's voice wasn't as confident as his, but damn if they didn't sound good together. By the second chorus, she was harmonizing with him, and Adam's beer was empty. He needed something stronger.

As expected, the duo received a roar of applause and cheers, along with a special shout-out from the cruise director, who took over the microphone to welcome everyone aboard. Hugh bowed and then clapped in Eve's direction before leading her into a twirl to the fawning delight of the occupants in the room.

She was laughing and flushed with the excitement of their performance. Although Adam beamed from seeing her enjoying herself and his heart filled with pride at her ability, it was all very clear that he was the third wheel to their duet. His smile faded, and they wove their way back to the cocktail table, Hugh's arm around her shoulders.

"You were amazing," Adam said when she reached him.

"Don't you mean, *Hugh* were amazing?" Hugh corrected, crossing his arms across his puffed-out chest. "Would you like to go next, soldier?"

Fucker. "No, I don't sing."

Hugh had the nerve to send him a satisfied smirk. "That's a shame." Turning to Eve, he said, "Remember that dodgy pub on the East End of London? We were there for a fancy dress party and you were in that cat suit. You were spectacular. You had everyone up on their feet requesting popular American songs. That one drunk bloke kept calling you 'Blondie.' And I don't know how that fight broke out, but it was classic, chairs flying. I grabbed you and we raced out the back just in time."

Eve laughed at the memory. "And that's when I decided to retire my karaoke hat to ensure world peace."

They were both laughing now, and Adam forced himself to join in, feeling acutely the outsider. He would have loved to have seen Eve in all her glory and been the one to protect her that night. Hell, he would have relished smashing a face or two to ensure her safety, starting with whoever was calling her "Blondie."

"Shall we do another ditty in a bit?"

"No," Eve answered firmly. "I really am tired. I think I'll just go back to my room for the night."

"Our room," Adam supplied, enjoying the way Hugh slanted his head to glare at him.

"Right, of course, that's what I meant," Eve corrected, reaching out to slip a delicate hand in Adam's. It fit perfectly, and he stilled himself to keep from squeezing tighter and pulling her closer like he wanted. But dammit, it felt so natural. How could she not feel it, too?

Dammit, he hadn't been imagining the desire that flared in her eyes at dinner. He would have to hold on to that hope, because corny or not, Eve was the missing piece in his life. He hadn't even known what he was looking for until she presented herself and the more he got to know her, the more sure he was that they were right for one another. Now, only if he could prove it to her.

"What did you ever see in that oxygen thief?" Adam asked the minute they entered their cabin. Although it had been on his mind, he hadn't meant to say it out loud, but too late now.

"I know, but he's not always like that. You don't know him."

"All right, then." He folded his arms across his chest, leaning on the closed bathroom door. "Let me take a whack at a profile on him. Please correct me if I'm wrong. He places considerable importance upon the material aspects of life. He has an eye for quality"—he looked pointedly at Eve—"desiring always the very best that money can buy, and not content with anything that is second best. He's quick to size up others based upon their physical appearance, their clothes, and whether they have achieved material success with the standards he has set in his own mind. He is opportunistic, and while likely overall still a good person, he puts himself first."

Eve opened and closed her mouth, and he fought the urge to lean in and lick her lips. Everything she was thinking was written on her lovely face. She was annoyed with him, but also conceded the truth. Was she this easy to read to everyone, or could he see what others couldn't? Hopefully, it was the latter.

"Fine," she admitted, kicking off her white heels. One flew forward by his feet, the other behind her, rolling underneath the desk. She lost a couple of inches, and damn if that didn't make him want her more. "That's him in a nutshell, but it's not all of him. He was drinking more than usual tonight, but he can be clever, adventurous, charming, debonair ..."

Adam lifted his hand to tell her to stop. He'd known drill sergeants with more charm than that guy. But if that was what she wanted, he'd be all of those things—and more. Way more. However, he hadn't intended to have her defend her ex, and he couldn't stomach listening to an endless list of praise. He needed to change tacks immediately. "Didn't you ask me to remind you that he's an asshole? Worse, a plagiarizing asshole?"

Her shoulders drooped, the fight leaving her as quickly as it arrived. "Ugh, you're right. Thank you." She collapsed onto one of the single beds, bouncing slightly in the process.

Their cabin seemed to have shrunk because the beds and Eve were all Adam could see. He tugged on the collar of his shirt, which suddenly seemed tight, too. He needed to get out of there. It was way too soon to make any kind of move or declaration. It was only their first day on board this floating disaster, and being her confidante was more than he'd hoped for already. Sure, he was planning to spend as much time as he could with her, getting to know one another better, but he hadn't accounted for nighttime, too.

Liar. All right, he'd envisioned a lot of nighttime activities, but those were fantasies, not reality. At least not yet. Being stuck in the same room was certainly a bonus and a big step in the right direction. An ex-fiancé, though, was a massive step back.

"Uh ..." He fumbled for words. "I think I'll go take a walk around the deck, see if I can actually get a signal to make a call."

"Okay," she said, looking up at him, her doe eyes full of concern. "Normally, I'm not such a party pooper, but we have an early day tomorrow and, to be honest, seeing Hugh out of the blue and this charade I stupidly forced us into has worn me out. I'm really sorry. This isn't fair to you. You didn't even want to be on this press trip, and now you can't even be yourself."

"I'm being myself," he defended. "Adoring you is easily done, Eve, and I meant every word that I said at dinner."

Her breath caught on a little hitch, so soft he shouldn't have noticed it. Of course, he did. He noticed everything about her. She continued to take him in for a moment, as if weighing whether or not he was telling the truth. "That was sweet," she said eventually, her smile soft and intimate.

He shrugged, feeling like an imbecile with leaded feet and a shirt that continued to choke him. "Good night," he said abruptly and louder than he had meant to. Gaining control of his legs, he managed to walk out the door when all he wanted to do was stay, looking at her forever. Now wasn't the time, though. He just hoped she'd give him the chance when it was.

10

Adam awoke the next day with morning wood, which in itself wasn't anything new. Having the woman that his dick was clamoring for only three feet away from him was. Groaning, he bit into his pillow and shifted to his side, physically turning away from Eve, a.k.a. temptation incarnate. Her parents had named her well.

Their alarm was set to go off any minute so they could get ready for their scheduled breakfast and tour of the galley with the head chef, followed by a selection of onboard activities that they could choose from. But first, he needed to collect himself and think of anything but Eve.

Football ... *good*. Eve in a football jersey and knee-high socks. *Nope*. The old nuns from his CCD class ... *better*. Eve kneeling in front of him. *Dammit!* Darfur. *That's more like it.* The pipe bomb that exploded steps away from the tank he'd been riding in. *Bam*. The dog with one ...

Ring! Ring!

Even though he'd been expecting it, the alarm jolted him as if he were still embedded with the troops. Clearly still groggy from sleep, Eve jumped much higher, coming out of the bed and looking around her unfamiliar surroundings in a haze. Although she was standing up, he could tell no one was home yet.

"It's okay," he whispered soothingly as he reached over for the phone, lifted it, and returned it to its cradle. "It's just the wake-up call they set for us."

She nodded, but her glassy eyes were still unfocused. Who knew she wasn't as bright and chipper first thing in the morning as she appeared to be all day? Why this unexpected contradiction only made her more appealing, he didn't know. He just loved having this private knowledge of her.

His gaze raked her from disheveled head to bare toes. *Good Lord!*

When he'd returned late last night from sipping a bourbon and brooding in the casino bar, she'd already been asleep. Thank goodness, because if he'd known she'd gone to bed in just a threadbare T-shirt that barely reached her hips and hot-pink, string-bikini panties, there was no way he'd have gotten one second of sleep last night.

He tried to keep his eyes on hers, but they kept straying down. If his face hadn't felt numb at the moment, he probably would have smiled over the fact that her tiny, neon underwear had a silly pineapple print. Of course she'd wear something adorably sunny like that and still make it look sexy. He bet she'd taste as sweet and tangy as the exotic fruit, too.

With no willpower before coffee, he couldn't prevent the fantasies that were taking hold. Images of him dropping to his knees in front of her and drawing the triangle swatch of cloth down with his teeth, nipping at her thighs as he let the flimsy cotton pool around her feet. And then, gently scraping his morning stubble slowly up the same path to taste her, licking open her seam from bottom to top.

Her abrupt inhale brought his eyes back up to hers, which were now clear from sleep and as wide as saucers. "I ... I better get dressed," she said, tugging down her T-shirt, which didn't hide much more from his current view. Belatedly, he averted his eyes, guilt washing over him as Eve dashed off to their tiny shared bathroom and locked the door behind her.

Holy crap!

Eve glared at her reflection in horror. It wasn't the first time she'd had a mind-blowing wet dream about Adam, but to wake up and see him eye-fucking her? She was practically dripping from his greedy stare, which had burned pleasure right to where she desired it most. It was as if someone had aimed a heat lamp right on her pussy.

Not to mention his disheveled hair and chiseled and tanned bare chest. Apparently, she'd slept next to an athlete. She hadn't expected the two solid-black, armband tattoos that circled his left bicep, but then again, he was badass enough to pull it off. And now she knew exactly where one of his scars was. Just below his pebbled nipple and dangerously close to his heart. The location sent a shiver of fear through her. To think he'd been so close to danger that shrapnel had hit him there. And now he was just a door away from her.

How was she possibly going to be able to ignore her growing attraction to him when they were sharing a two-hundred-square-foot cabin?

And thanks to her stupidity yesterday, she'd ensured their close proximity in her attempts to keep Hugh away. Basically, she'd substituted one danger to her heart with another. When had her life become a soap opera?

The Celsius shower knob alternated the water temperature from freezing to boiling, so she opted for cold, to cool off. It didn't work. She yearned for Adam to come in and join her. Although, now that she had taken a good look at him, she wondered if it would even be physically possible for both of them to fit in here, given the tiny shower stall and his impressive size. He probably had to hunch just to wash up when he was alone in here.

Toweling off, Eve put on another one of her wrinkle-free, travel sundresses. Taking a deep, steadying breath, she stepped out into the cabin to find Adam already gone. *Phew.* The relief twirling in her stomach mixed with disappointment, and the combination left her unsteady as she gathered her notepad and key card. What ridiculous plot twist was today going to bring?

11

By the time Eve joined their scheduled galley tour, Adam stood at the front of the line asking questions about the cruise line's sustainability choices and how they avoided unnecessarily wasting food. Despite the interesting topic, she concentrated on his thick, full lips moving and his angular face. He towered over the kitchen staff and reporters by several inches, but the way he casually stuffed one hand in the pocket of his shorts gave him a boyish, trusting look that drew everyone in. Hell, she wanted to float closer—much closer—but Eve shoved those thoughts aside.

As if he felt her eyes on him, Adam turned toward her and flashed a wide smile that had her heart pounding faster. The intimate moment broke when the crew shifted to another area in the kitchens and continued their tour.

At first, she was relieved to be bringing up the rear, but then Hugh stood beside her. Instead of taking notes or having a recorder out like Adam, he rolled his eyes and followed, seeming disinterested.

"Fifteen hundred pounds of flour is used each day to create the ship's fresh-baked bread, homemade pasta, and pastry shop treats," said the chef with a thick, Italian accent. "We store eighteen thousand bottles of wine and champagne in our wine cellars."

His vino fun fact caused a stir of admiration from the group, and the man nodded proudly. Eve jotted down the numbers. Their subscribers would be equally impressed.

"Thank you, everyone," Natalie called as she passed around flyers. "Here is a list of open activities available for you throughout today's at-sea day. We recommend that you try at least two of the highlighted activities chosen by the cruise committee, but please select whatever is of interest to you and your audiences."

With that, the reporters dispersed. Eve lingered a moment longer to review the itinerary, wavering between the champagne art auction, napkin-folding demonstration, or ballroom instruction.

Considering all of the onboard activities being offered, she did not expect to find Adam twirling an elderly, blue-haired lady in the ballroom. *With a revolver and Mrs. White.* Eve laughed to herself as she took in the scene. There were over a dozen white-haired women on the dance floor. She debated stepping backward, as if she had never entered the circular room currently playing a Tom Jones number, but she found herself moving forward for a better view.

The music came to a stop as an older couple in matching, sequined uniforms entered the dance floor and clapped their hands, calling for everyone's attention.

"Today, we will be learning the Cha Cha," the male instructor announced. "Now, if the ladies would step to one side of the dance floor and gents on the other, we'll model the right direction for the steps first, and then we'll start off as a group. So, guys, keep your eyes on me, and ladies, please follow my lovely partner, Blanche."

Speaking to the crowd, the instructors broke down the triple steps needed to properly perform the Latin dance, demonstrating the perspective from both the male and female positions. "One-two-cha-cha-cha."

Eve stayed in the back of the group, following along as best she could, which admittedly was nowhere near her best. She'd stepped forward when the line of women in front of her stepped back, bumping into not one, but two dancers. After several more repetitions of the steps, she was almost getting the hang of it.

"Marvelous," Blanche called out. "Please select a partner, and let us continue our Cha Cha lesson as it should be done—as a duo."

The senior vixen Adam was dancing with earlier was heading in his direction to snag him once again. Springing into action, Eve picked up her steps, practically shoving the poor lady out of the way in order to claim the dance. If God were a female, Eve was surely going to lose points for her competitive instinct, and for not respecting her elders, too. Eve shrugged the irksome thought away. After all, all was fair in love and war. *Love? Slow your roll, girl!*

Given Adam's alarmed expression at her abrupt arrival, Eve wasn't sure who was more surprised, the jilted septuagenarian or him. Hell, she was, too, but she'd acted on impulse. If anyone was going to be cocooned in Adam's arms, it was going to be her. For this dance, at least, and only for the story's sake, she qualified.

"Um ... there you are, sunshine," he said, sounding bemused.

"Have you been looking for me?" she asked, hoping it was so.

He smirked. "All my life."

He was only teasing, but damn if his words and smile

didn't send butterflies dancing around in her belly. She cleared her throat and reminded herself to be professional. "May I have this dance?" she asked with a smile, placing her hand in his. "Just please go easy on my toes."

He nodded. "It would be my honor, my lady, and I promise your li'l piggies are safe with me as long as you don't tread on mine."

"Oh really?" she asked, liking his cocky tone and the way his arm confidently snaked around the small of her back, pulling her closer. His assured hold, and the beckoning warmth of his chest, had her insides melting and her stomach already doing a Cha Cha of its own. She sucked in a fortifying breath in an effort to keep it together. Still, his left eyebrow arched knowingly at her action.

"I might just surprise you," he said smoothly.

"You always do," she admitted, enjoying his smile and finding herself leaning closer than was necessary to learn the moves.

Notwithstanding the distraction that was Adam, Eve held her own in his arms the first minute or so of the dance routine. The steps were thankfully easier to follow than the ones from the Zumba class Jada had managed to drag her to on their lunch hour. Eve's first and last time going. She faltered when they added a spin to their Cha Cha, and she mistakenly stepped forward instead of back. Adam, meanwhile, was unruffled with each new addition and moved with ease, his sure stance and steps almost putting the ship's own instructors to shame.

She couldn't help but throw him an accusing look. "Why are you so good?"

He grinned, leading her back in the right direction after her misstep. "There's a lot about me that you don't know."

True, and not for the first time, she wanted to learn all

his secrets. The possibilities had her pulse racing. That and the fact that his wicked grins were starting to have an effect on her, so much so that she had to count her steps out loud to stay in rhythm. "Seriously, how are you doing this?"

Instead of answering, he had the nerve to dip her. Deliberately, she trampled on his foot, which only made him smile more. "I grew up with a single mom," he eventually said with a laugh. "When I was in middle school, she signed us both up for continuing education dance classes at the community center. Of course, I bitched and moaned at first, but then she convinced me that a man who can dance always had women lining up to be whisked off their feet. And I guess she was right because look, here you are."

With that revelation, he expertly directed her into a complicated spin that the instructors hadn't shared with the group. The applause that broke out around them saved Eve from having to admit that his mother was undeniably right. Mashed up against him, her body was humming with a sexual awareness that threatened to consume her. Reluctantly, they broke apart, and she bowed to the small crowd, expelling a breathless laugh.

From the corner of her eye, she caught Hugh eyeing them. She hadn't been aware he was even in the room. He met her gaze with one of his charming looks, which now did nothing for her.

"Switch partners!" the male instructor called out, and before either of them could grumble at the order, Hugh was pulling her away.

"You know how to Cha Cha?" Adam called out to their retreating form.

"But of course. I'm English," Hugh professed over his shoulder. "We grow up ballroom dancing. Just ask Ginger here about our moonlit dance in Bora Bora."

Adam's scowl indicated that he didn't want to hear about that night, and to be honest, neither did she. Despite that night's romantic setting, all Eve remembered was Hugh pointing out the other couples who were better. No, that wasn't fair. They'd also walked along the beach, holding hands and humming the melody afterward.

"It's nice to have you back in my arms," Hugh murmured, leading her into the dance routine. "Like old times."

His familiar voice caused her heart to skip a beat. Whatever she was about to say lodged in her throat as a wave of nostalgia hit her. Hugh's customary musk scent invaded her nostrils, prompting happier memories, too.

"I'm over you," she declared, but even to her own ears, her voice had sounded sad.

"I keep telling myself the same thing each day. Is it working?"

She nodded more firmly. While it was comfortable being in his arms again, it wasn't like before. Yes, he looked exactly the same, but everything felt different. No more sizzle. No butterflies in her stomach, no tingling from their touch where their hands met. And despite the bittersweet memories flooding her mind, plenty of the unhappy ones were there, too. "I've already mourned our relationship, Hugh. I'm not where you left me at all."

"*You* left me, not the other way around," he corrected, his tone defensive.

One of the hardest things she'd ever done was moving out of his place. "You pulled away long before I did. Besides, you didn't even notice that I'd left until after your book tour ended."

His grip on her tightened. "I was on the road. How was I supposed to know you'd packed up your things?"

She laughed bitterly. "Maybe the fact that we hadn't talked in weeks?"

"It's a rocking step, not a stomp," he clipped out, his wistful tone from before gone. "Slow, quick, quick, slow, quick, quick. Come on, this is the easiest of the ballroom dances." And there was her not measuring up to his standards. She didn't need Adam reminding her that Hugh was an asshole after all. He was doing that himself. "I have to say, I'm surprised to find you ... um ... dancing with someone else already," he added, sounding hurt.

"Already?" Shocked, she tripped over her own foot. "If you don't want to see me dancing with somebody, then don't show up. Don't start caring about me now."

"Can we please talk privately?" he pleaded. "I can fix this."

"Switch!" the ballroom instructors called out in unison.

Yes, it was definitely time for a switch. No more going 'round and 'round with Hugh. She'd give him that private talk he desired and the closure they both needed.

"Our schedule is jam-packed the rest of the day," she said, stepping away and wrapping her arms protectively around her ribcage. "I'm sure you're done pretending to do any of the planned activities, but I can meet you before dinner."

"My cabin?" he asked, his face lighting up.

Eve shook her head. "The Wheelhouse Bar, and it's just to talk," she amended, before moving to the guy patiently waiting to her left. Pity for her it wasn't Adam again.

While doing a turn with her new partner, she swiveled her head around the room but could no longer find Adam among the crowd at all. She felt that ache in the pit of her stomach that told her she cared. She gritted her teeth, as if to grind the unwanted and irksome feeling away. She was foolishly buying into their fake romance. Hadn't she learned anything from her first disastrous go-around with a colleague? She'd let love—well, what she'd thought was love—cloud her better judgment. And now her former fiancé was winning awards and topping the bestseller charts for a book she'd help write. She wasn't going to be fooled by a handsome face again, even if he could dance and send electric sizzles throughout her body with just a smile or a witty remark. No siree, Adam.

12

Eve halted in front of the entrance to the Wheelhouse Bar and zipped up her hoodie over the black-sequined evening dress that showed off the girls without looking slutty. She'd earmarked the gown for tonight's formal group dinner scheduled at the ship's award-winning steakhouse. Supper would be a more intimate setting, since the restaurant was reservation-only and came with an additional upcharge per person. Usually, passengers saved these extra dining experiences for special occasions or skipped them altogether to dine in the gratis dining rooms or buffets only.

But first, she had another intimate meetup to go to, and she didn't want it to seem as if she were dressing up for it or *him*—thus the bulky coverup.

Eve took a deep, fortifying breath before entering the lounge. Spotting Hugh in a private, c-shaped alcove in the back, she snaked her way past the other tables and patrons with as much willingness as a woman about to have a mammogram.

The jazz band on the nearby stage played a melancholy

beat that matched her turbulent emotions as she stared at the man she once loved. The ache in her chest might be an old pain, but it still stung. At one time, her heart would have been pounding with excitement and she'd have raced to him. Now she stared at someone else entirely in his place. A man she could not respect, one with more ambition than tenderness. All the same, there was still a part of her that wanted to cry. Not because she missed him, but more that she mourned the dreams she'd built around him.

Hugh stood as she neared, a gentlemanly move that, at one time, would have melted her, as did most of his social graces. She slumped unceremoniously into the worn, brown-leather seat next to him. It was closer than she wanted to be, but the table for two didn't offer much elbow room.

His gaze zeroed in on her zip-up sweatshirt. "Cold?"

She ignored the critique. "You wanted to talk. So, talk."

"Hmm," he murmured, reaching for the stainless-steel ice bucket resting on the table. "I ordered us a bottle of Prosecco. You were always partial to it."

He was right. Her feelings hadn't changed toward the bubbly, just for him. He poured each flute at an angle with expertise, the tide of foam reaching the rim but never spilling over. It wouldn't dare.

"Thank you," she said, accepting the glass and sipping the golden drink. She wasn't one to drink to calm her nerves, but at the moment, it was doing just that. Liquid courage at its best.

Hugh cleared his throat, the silent scolding for having taken a sip before they toasted clear in his eyes. "To old friends, good times, and new beginnings," he said, clinking his flute against hers.

To new friends and better times, she was tempted to spit

back, but that seemed churlish. Instead, she took another sip and eyed him warily. "Why start now? These grand gestures. Showing up on this trip? It's been months since I left, and even longer since we were last together."

"It's not for lack of trying to get in touch with you," he said, straightening.

"Missed calls are hardly the same as coming to talk face-to-face with me."

"You left while I was in the middle of my press tour," he repeated, looking at her as if she had horns. "I had appearances already booked throughout Europe and the States. It wouldn't have been fair to the marketing department to cancel and return to Florida just because my love life had hit a speed bump."

That *speed bump* had only been her heart, but whatever. "Of course, how silly of me," she muttered, letting an elbow rest on the table just because she knew it would annoy him.

"Well, it's over now," he said with a dismissive shrug.

She nodded. "Yes, it is."

"I was referring to the press junket," he clarified.

"I wasn't," she said, laughing sardonically and taking another deep sip.

"Doesn't it count that I'm here now? Besides, I have something for you." He reached below the u-shaped table and handed her a legal-size, manila envelope.

Was she being served? The thought had her fighting back a chuckle. Placing her flute on the coaster in front of her, she accepted the folder. "What is it?" she asked automatically, slipping out the papers that were inside.

He crossed his arms and gave her an eager grin. "Read it."

She spotted her name among the words and looked back up at him, dumbfounded.

"It's a dedication and an acknowledgement for your work on my book."

His book. *Humph.* "I can see that, but *our* guide has been published for a while now. *This* is just a piece of paper."

"Yes, but that is what will go into the *next* edition. I already worked it out with the publisher this time."

"A second edition?" she echoed.

"I know, isn't it great?" he asked, beaming with pride and taking a celebratory sip from his own glass. "The guide is doing so well that they are planning a second printing. In fact, the publishing house would like me to update it and issue a new edition every year. I could be the next Rick Steeves, but younger and better, naturally. Just think, we can work together like before and discover new places. We can visit the Italian vineyards where they make Prosecco, a grand tour." He scooted closer and scooped up her hand, squeezing it tight before continuing. "It could be an all-expenses-paid honeymoon around the world."

"How romantic," she said drolly, but Hugh didn't seem to notice the lack of excitement in her tone or how she slipped her hand out from his grasp.

"Right? I'm giving you the world, Eve, literally. We'll be a traveling team again. This could lead to television deals, podcasts, an exclusive tour business, you name it!"

"A team implies that not only the workload is shared, but also the credit. My name should damn well be listed on the spine as well."

"Come on, we've been over this. My name is the reason why people are even buying the guide. There's no reason to confuse the reader with petty nuances on the business side of publishing. You'll have my name soon, anyway. Besides, there is no I in team, right?"

Yes, but as she always liked to point out whenever

people trotted out that trite, motivational line, there was a *me*, and it would always be Hugh, never her.

"I'm already part of a team and writing under my own name as well," she pointed out.

He snorted. "For the local newspaper? That was just to pay the bills while you did real writing with me. And with that G.I. Joe? He belongs in Washington. For fuck's sake, he's never been on a cruise before."

"He doesn't claim to know everything, and it's freakin' refreshing. Either way, both of our names will be appearing on the byline, at least. I also enjoy writing for the *Tribune*."

"It's not the same as a book, and I told you, you *will* be credited in the next edition." Hugh slapped papers on the table.

"Too little, too late, Hugh, and you know very well I should have more than a mere mention."

"I'm compromising here. Maybe you should, too." He crossed his arms over his chest. "Can't you see that I've changed?"

More like an empty gesture, but she didn't want to keep bickering. "Maybe you have"—she waved between them—"but so have I."

"So, that's it?" he asked, not bothering to hide the irritation in his tone. "You're turning down my proposal so that you can be a columnist for some little paper?"

She slammed down her glass. If there had still been any liquid left in it, she would have been tempted to splash the contents in his face. "It wasn't much of a proposal, and I have many plans for my life. They just no longer include *you*. I'm not where you left me at all."

"You don't say," he said, pursing his lips into a thin smile. "To me, it looks like you are nowhere at all."

She stood to leave, but his hand tugged at her elbow, forcing her to turn back.

"You realize I can find someone else to join me, don't you?"

"I hope she doesn't mind being the wind beneath your wings because that's not me. Not anymore." She released her anger and tension out with her next breath. "I do wish you the best, but it's not with me."

"But you are the best," he said, his voice sounding small.

She couldn't stop the slight pang of guilt and compassion in the pit of her stomach from his words. "Yes," she said, standing tall, "but you realized it too late. Goodbye, Hugh."

If she had needed closure, then this meeting had provided it, once and for all. She wasn't throwing away her future happiness. No, she'd just taken the right step toward what was best for her, and that meant leaving Hugh in the past.

13

Adam paced inside their cabin, which technically meant he was only walking a couple steps in each direction, spastically shuffling around like someone who couldn't find their glasses when they were right on top of their empty head.

He'd had to escape earlier. He felt like a dumbass, fighting over the chance to dance with her. Of course, he was willing to fight for Eve, but not like some grade-school boy. He didn't want to pressure her, either, and if he was really being truthful, his pride refused to be so available, too.

Still, he'd assumed he'd have caught up with her by now. Their itinerary had a break for everyone to recharge. From the debris of products on the counter, and her scent lingering in the air, Eve had returned at some point earlier. He must have just missed her. But now, dinner was in about twenty minutes and she still hadn't reappeared.

Adam tugged on his bow tie and tried not to picture her in the arms of Hugh. The image gave him heartburn. Rummaging through his army-issued toiletry bag, he popped two acid relief tabs in his mouth and chewed the chalky discs.

Man up! He'd trained alongside the military, gone on their missions. He had more discipline than this. Being around Eve, though, was like heading into a demilitarized zone. He simply had no protection when it came to her. It was both thrilling and terrifying.

A sudden smile split his face. How long had that feeling been missing from his life? All work and no play had made him a mere shadow of his old self. The man he'd been before war and responsibilities came crashing down on him and the strings of his former freedom were pulled tight.

Feeling claustrophobic in his tux, he hauled air into his lungs and was just about to rip the stifling thing off when the electronic click from the keycard lock had him whirling around. Whatever clever remark he'd been rehearsing for when Eve arrived disappeared the moment she entered ... crying.

Instinctually, he moved forward, opening his arms to her. His heart skipped a beat when she walked into his embrace as naturally as breathing and rubbed her forehead into the nook of his shoulder. He hugged her, gently swaying in what he hoped was a soothing motion.

"There, there," he said, fairly sure he'd never said those words before, but it seemed like something he was supposed to say. He couldn't take her tears. He could barely handle her smiles.

She took two deep breaths, her shoulders lifting up and down in the process. Shifting, he moved her toward the bed and sat down with Eve still in his arms. She seemed more in control now, no longer crying, but she wasn't letting go of him, either.

Cupping her face, he brushed away the lingering

teardrops on her pinkened cheeks, which felt like wet silk. He didn't think it was possible, but her eyes were even bluer when welled up with tears. He hated that she had to cry for him to see such an outrageous shade, though.

"What did he do?" he asked, unable to wait any longer to know why she was upset.

She pulled away but stayed slumped next to him, new tears rolling down her cheeks. "Nothing."

Such a ridiculous answer made him shake his head. "Nothing? I don't think so."

"I'm fine," she said with an exasperated shrug.

"No woman is ever *fine* when they say that word, especially when crying."

"Fine," she said, letting out a breathy chuckle. "He proposed again."

A protective reflex had his arm rising back up to settle on her shoulders. "Did you accept?" he somehow managed to ask over the grapefruit-size lump in his throat.

She stiffened. "Of course not. Been there, done that."

"Then why are you crying?"

"Because he finally acknowledged my work, something he should have done ages ago, and now it's meaningless. *We* were meaningless, and I don't know, I guess I'm upset for having ever loved him in the first place. For being such a pushover, for not fighting harder for my share of the credit, and for not knowing my value overall. For a lot of things."

Unable to resist, he brushed back her hair and chucked her under the chin. "But you didn't put up with it, Eve. You broke it off when you knew it wasn't right. Sometimes it's easier to simply stay than to go. That takes guts, and I'm so proud of you for knowing your worth because you are way too good to let anyone hold you back."

The bluest of blue eyes stared up at him, and he gulped

for air. She used the back of her palms to swipe away the last vestige of her tears. "You ... you don't even know me."

"Sure I do, but I do want to get to know you better." And then he'd really be screwed because the more he discovered, and the more he touched her, the more he seemed to fall. "And as for that damn book, fuck it. You should write your own. You already know what it takes to write a successful guide, and you can do it in your own voice and style, not his insincere one." Nodding along to his own idea, he added, "As soon as we get back, I'll introduce you to my publisher. We'll send him your writing samples, along with a backgrounder on you."

"You would do that for me?"

He'd do so much more that it was laughable. "Consider it done."

"Your editor doesn't focus on travel writing, though."

"No, but the greater publishing house does. They'd be lucky to have someone as talented as you. Besides, you're not the only one in my debt," he teased. "They owe me, too."

She emitted a soft, breathy laugh. "I appreciate it, really. Hugh guarded his publishing relationships like the last Cadbury Creme Egg on Easter."

He laughed at the silly image. "I'm happy to share all my contacts, baby. It's not like it would hurt me to see you succeed. There's room in the publishing world for all of us, but be warned ..." He trailed off, tilting her chin up so their gazes locked. He was glad to see that her eyes were less red now with no more tears present. "I never, and I repeat, I *never* share my Cadbury Creme Eggs. Sorry, you'll have to get your own."

She giggled. "Good, because I'm not giving you any of mine, either."

He prayed they were still only talking about the chocolate holiday eggs. Although, he already knew he'd cave if it came to those, too. She was all the sweetness he'd ever need in life.

Her voice broke him out of his fanciful thoughts. "I ... uh ... I haven't told anyone yet, but I have been working on an outline for a travel guide that is geared toward female travelers. A girlfriend's guide to traveling abroad. Safety tips and even clothing suggestions. *'The Femme Traveler.'*"

"That's perfect." *You're perfect.* The words popped immediately to mind, but he didn't voice them. "Sounds like a great niche, too."

"I just—"

"What?" he asked, seeing the turmoil in her readable face.

"I'm afraid I might not be able to do it on my own."

"That's bullshit!" he said, not meaning for his words to come out so forcefully. "I'm sure Hugh made you feel that way, but that's nonsense. You know you're talented, and hell, he probably can't write without you, not the other way around."

"You're right, I know you're right," she said, bobbing her head.

"Damn straight." He had to take a deep breath for a moment to calm his outrage and desire to strangle Hugh.

She shifted toward him, the bed dipping in the process, bringing his hip against hers. Her lips twitched into a sly, sideways grin. "And what would I owe you this time for using your influence once again?"

He was about to say she owed him nothing, but the heat rolling off her body had him pausing. Still, he couldn't untie his tongue to say anything coherent.

Her mouth formed a sexy O as she searched his face and

he bent down. She tilted her head up toward him. Encouraged, he paused right before their lips touched. Hovering only a breath away, it felt as if her mouth was a magnet drawing him in, his neck aching from resisting her electric pull. "May I?" he croaked.

Her lips eagerly met his in answer. Slowly, he brushed his mouth back and forth, getting to know the feel of her thin but tender lips, which parted on a slight moan. That did it. He lifted his hands to her cheeks and pulled her in deeper. He needed this kiss more than he needed air at the moment. All the passion he felt came pouring out as he traced the corners of her mouth and tangled his tongue with hers. She tasted of champagne and Eve. He let out a low growl that mingled with her sigh of pleasure.

She surprised the heck out of him when she nipped at his bottom lip and took over the kiss. Rising up to better meet his height, she straddled his lap, bringing herself even closer. He dropped his hands from her face and squeezed her tight, one arm slung around her hips to cup her ass and the other roaming her back to feel and memorize as much as he could of her.

"Jesus," he whispered against her mouth, rubbing his lips over hers as he pulled back a millimeter, still unable to remove his hands that stroked the small of her back. He should have, though, since tracing the dip of her spine only inflamed the desire sparking throughout his own body.

He'd been about to stop when she jumped back first, slightly shoving him away. "Dinner!" she squeaked, scrambling to her feet and looking around the room as if taking in her surroundings for the first time since she'd entered earlier. "We have dinner," she repeated, smoothing over her hair and readjusting her stunning, black dress. Not meeting his eyes, she slipped her shoes back on and darted for the exit.

Adam was left on the bed, trying to restart his heart.

14

Eve spent the rest of their media dinner trying not to recall their unexpected kiss, but found herself sucking on her still-tingling bottom lip all the same. Thankfully, Hugh hadn't bothered to show up, not that she could blame him this time post-rejection. With Adam arriving after her, they were seated at separate tables entirely.

Pamela beamed when Adam sat next to her, fading Eve's earlier relief into jealousy. It was absurd—she had no business being envious or even wanting him in the first place. Her brain was shooting off alarms louder than the emergency drill back on their first day, yet her stupid, bruised heart was experiencing all the feels. When would she ever learn?

Speaking of that emergency alarm, though, something had been nagging her about it. Pushing her salad around with her tiny fork, she recalled how Adam had jumped when the ringing went off, way more than anyone else in the room. She doubted it was because of the intimate moment they'd been sharing. No, the split second of fear that flashed in his steely eyes indicated something else. Despite whatever had been triggered in him, he'd also stepped in front of her instinctually. Both his protective gesture and his silent pain had drawn her closer than any conversation they'd had. She'd wanted to bear-hug him and make him forget whatever demons had taken over.

Looking up from her plate, she wasn't surprised when her gaze locked with Adam's from across the tables. Although she'd tried to ignore the intense pull, she'd been aware of him, like always. Was it the same for him? Ever since their trip started, he'd evidently given in to whatever forces were at work between them.

Rolling back her shoulders, she sat up straighter. Fine. Her resolve would just have to be strong enough for the both of them.

A slow, crooked smile tugged at Adam's full lips, and he shook his head ever so slightly in ... in contradiction to her stance? In warning?

Eve resisted the urge to stick her tongue out in response, but his snicker left her wondering if he knew that, too. Instead, she stabbed blindly at the new plate of food that had been placed in front of her. Stubbornly, she broke their gaze, barely tasting whatever it was she was eating.

"A penny for your thoughts?" He asked, making it sound like a dare rather than a common idiom.

There was something that felt so right about sitting beside him, talking to him, eating together. She forced her attention back to his question when he looked down at her.

"Nothing of consequence," she said with a shrug, taking the coward's way out.

Declining the group's offer to watch a comedy act after their meal, Eve returned to their cabin alone. Adam headed off to who knew where with his phone clutched in his hand. Although she wanted to be alone, her gut twisted in longing.

Her impractical thoughts were as wishy-washy as the waves outside their balcony, which explained why her stomach felt just as rocky, right?

With a sigh, she belly-flopped onto her designated bed and buried her face into the fluffy pillow. It was going to be a long night of replaying their kiss and remembering how right it felt to be in Adam's arms, despite how wrong it would inevitably turn out. She shook her head to ward off the warm feelings invading her. He was just another coworker destined to ruin her career and break her heart.

15

"We need to talk about last night," Eve affirmed the second Adam walked into their cabin the next morning.

He tossed his headphones on the desk. "What about it?" he asked with a shrug, doing his best not to laugh at her startled face.

Adam had woken hours earlier but couldn't fall back asleep with Eve so close and so much of her on his mind. As quietly as he could, he'd pulled on athletic clothes and headed up to the fitness center. He watched the sunrise through the panoramic windows while striding on the treadmill. Easily the nicest view he'd ever had while working out. Afterward, he utilized the locker room to get ready for their port day in Mexico.

"You know," she said, flailing her arms about. "What went on here before dinner."

"Oh?" He masked his own facial features, but her eyes, on the other hand, almost doubled in size.

"We kissed! And not the fake kind this time."

"Hmm ... fake, real. You're going to have to refresh my memory," he teased, striding purposefully forward.

Her hands came up to meet his chest, forming a wall instead of a caress. "Nice try. So, you're just going to pretend it didn't happen?"

He shook his head, unable to control his wicked grin. "Nope. I'm very much trying to make it happen again."

"It can never happen again," she said with conviction.

He froze, her depressing remark sobering his playful mood. "Why not?"

"You know why not."

"No, I don't. We're great together."

"We *work* together."

He shrugged. "So? It's not like we report to one another. A lot of couples meet at work."

"Trust me. It won't end well. I'm speaking from experience."

Wanting to shake her, he shoved a hand through his hair in frustration instead, taking advantage of the stall tactic to better select his words. "Let me get this straight. That selfish prick's mistakes are now ruining it for me?"

"Ruining what? This is just a made-up relationship, remember?" she asked, smacking at the heart he was wearing on his sleeve. "Besides, I don't know what's even gotten into you lately. You must have cabin fever or something. I've known you, what, almost two years, and you've never been this ... this way on land."

"What way? Interested? I've always been into you, but you were in a relationship when we met and then newly out of one, so I was trying to give you time and space to figure things out." He motioned around the room. "We've run out of space."

Not even a smile at his confession. He wanted to growl

when she shook her adorable head at him once more. "No way. You've never looked at me like—"

"Like I wanted to throw you down on your desk and fuck you?"

She sucked in a shocked breath. "Yes." She exhaled, her face flushing. She swallowed slowly, and the movement had him gulping, too, and stepping forward.

"Then you're not the observant reporter I thought you were. But then again, I'm no amateur. I've become an expert at stealing glances and going out of my way each day just to get a glimpse of your gorgeous face." Unable to resist, he brushed her wavy, blonde hair back from her aforementioned face and let his fingers skim against her reddened cheeks.

"That's not true. You're spinning things. Y-you're always mean to me."

He immediately dropped his hand. "How am I mean to you?"

"Fine, not mean, exactly," she conceded with a head bob, "but constantly teasing me and suggesting edits to my work, or poking fun at how I described the freakin' sunset, even."

"Bold, brilliant, and rich in color. The sun fell asleep, using the mountain as a blanket, shielding its full intensity from view," he said, quoting her work back. "I was impressed, that's all."

"You were?" she asked, her mouth gaping. "I ... you even managed to somehow change the desktop wallpaper on my office computer to a mountain sunset."

Laughing now, he could barely get out his reply. "Oh baby, didn't your parents ever warn you about the boys who tease girls on the playground and their real reason behind it?"

"Sure, but that's not what you were doing."

"It wasn't? Do you know the strings I had to pull with IT to even do that?" He stepped closer, stopping short when she backed up once more, her back coming into contact with a full-length, wall mirror.

Never the one to cower, despite being backed into a corner quite literally, Eve placed her hands on her hips in evident frustration and stepped forward. The movement drew his attention to her reflection and the stretchy, black leggings she was wearing, which clung to all her curves. Not to mention how her tight pants lifted her lush ass even higher, making it perfect for a man's hands. His hands, to be precise, and right at his grabbing level, too. He had to ball his fists into the flimsy pockets of his mesh shorts to keep from reaching out and testing his height theory.

"Um ..." He gulped. "Are you sure you want to wear that?"

She glanced down at her attire. Her brows furrowed. "Why? What's wrong with it?"

"It's ... uh ... awfully sexy for a rainforest hike and zip-line excursion."

"This? They're just yoga pants."

"Then I need to start taking yoga classes if this is what women are stretching in. What *you* are bending in. Damn."

"Wait," she said, twisting to glance at her reflection. "Do you think it might give Hugh the wrong idea?"

"Well, it's giving *me* several ideas, and not one of them involves leaving this room and going into the Caribbean jungle. Although, I'm sure if you give me a few seconds, my imagination could run wild there, too."

She rolled her eyes, obviously assuming once more he was only "teasing."

"But this is my go-to outdoor outfit when traveling. It doesn't wrinkle, has built-in UPF, and the extra coverage keeps the bugs from biting. So, if he's turned on, tough. Let him suffer."

Adam couldn't stop his own groan of suffering. "Me, too?"

Her breathy laugh only teased him further. "Oh, please," she drawled. "I'm sure you can handle it."

"I would love to handle *you*," he grumbled.

"The shower is right there," she said, pointing a dainty finger that he wanted to nip at. "Just set it to cold."

"Mmmm. Join me in it, and we can make it a hot one."

She merely glared at his suggestion.

"All right, all right," he said, putting up his hands in mock defense.

"I wish you never said anything," she muttered, glancing at the mirror again and pirouetting. "Now I'm worried he'll think I was trying to dress sexy. Maybe at some point during our tour, you can comment about how much you love me in these pants—"

"I do!"

She ignored his comment and continued her train of thought. "That way, he'll think I wore it for you."

"I wish," he quipped. "Fine, but then you—"

"Owe you?" she supplied with yet another eye roll. "Yeah, I know! Once I'm back home, I'll be sure and order these tights in your size."

"Cute," he admitted. "Just like you in those pants. Now, let's get your cute butt out this door, or I'm going to change your mind about dating a coworker. Actually, I plan to do that regardless. Just consider this a stay of execution." Her glower and pitiful attempt at appearing fierce had him biting back a smile.

"Not going to happen, Seager. I've been fooled by a pretty face before."

His eyebrows shot up. "You think I'm pretty?"

"Not the point, and no, you're too masculine to be called pretty."

"So, I'm masculine?" he asked, backing her up against the mirror once more.

"Ugh. Needing a compliment, are we?"

"Yes," he murmured, leaning in to peck at the curve of her neck, just below her ear, and inhaling her sweet scent. "Do you have more?"

She sighed, leaning in to him for the barest of seconds before shoving at his chest. "You're the most irr—"

"Irresistible man you've ever met?" he supplied before she could even finish her comment, which was obviously not going to be flattering.

Oomph. She shoved at his gut and ducked out from under his arm. Laughing, he threw his arms wide and moved out of her way. Shooting him an exasperated glare through squinted eyes, Eve opened the front door without looking back.

Adam was left with no choice but to follow her tightly clad body sashaying down the narrow hallway to the elevator bank. It was going to be a long, painful day.

He couldn't wait.

16

Zip-lining with the salt of the ocean in the air and fragrant flowers filling his senses was much different than the time Adam had careened off a rooftop in Afghanistan with a makeshift rope and a questionable carabiner he prayed wouldn't spring open. This time, without his ears ringing from a nearby blast and the fear of death minimal, soaring fifty feet off the ground was exhilarating.

Their equipment, helmet, and safety clips were all top-notch, and no one was shooting at them. He still had to watch where he stepped, though—he wasn't about to be the goof who fell off the narrow platforms. The massive termite hills that were caked onto the sides of the trees were like their own mines to be avoided. He couldn't fault Eve's squeal when she'd narrowly swung by one such formation. Hugh had chuckled, even though he'd made a wide berth when he stepped off the ledge for his turn. Adam enjoyed a few minutes of imagining Hugh's head going into one of the bug-filled protrusions. Now, that would make for an interesting sidebar to his story.

Still, the tour group ahead of them, which consisted of

several seniors who were far from being in the best of health, had all made it to the final canopy point safely before being loaded back into their shuttle bus to return to port. Adam's adventure wasn't over yet, though. Their tour package included a hike to see the famous cliff divers fly into the waters below.

The mile-long climb was easy. Not staring at Eve in her yoga pants as she trekked ahead of him, however, wasn't. The path was single file, and being the gentleman that he was, he of course told Eve to go first while blocking Hugh from going next in line. The putz grumbled behind him the whole way.

At one point, Hugh called out some name of a plant or flower to Eve and tried to shove past Adam, but she simply yelled back, "Yup, I saw that." She didn't seem to be giving Hugh any chance today to be friendly.

Adam smacked another mosquito that landed on his forearm, wishing he wasn't in swim trunks and a thick, cotton T-shirt, but rather something more protective and airier. Hugh, the traveling maverick, had on a thin, long-sleeve, sun-protective shirt that had a wind tunnel opening in the back. Adam would have to recommend the extra protection and bug spray to his readers. His readers? Never had he considered providing advice in his pieces before. He'd been taught to be impartial, factual. Suggesting what someone should wear had never entered his realm of writing possibility before.

The brush cleared, and so did Adam's thoughts as the vast ocean view appeared before them. He stood still at first, transfixed. Feeling a pull, he stepped closer to the steep edge than was probably safe. A pebble plummeted into the aqua-blue water below, which slapped at the jagged edges of the rocky cliff. The color of the ocean matched Eve's captivating eyes.

"Close your eyes," Eve said in a whisper beside him.

He wanted to turn to look at her, but he did as he was told.

"Take a deep breath."

Again, he did as she instructed, his bare forearm brushing against hers as he dragged in a deep gulp of air. The mere touch sent goose bumps down his arm.

"Keep your eyes closed," she warned.

"Are you going to push me off the cliff?"

Her sweet laughter at his question drowned out the waves and the sounds of other journalists nearby. It felt like it was just the two of them in that moment with the sun beating down, their scents mixing. "Because if you'd truly rather write alone, there are better ways to go about it."

"Shh. Take another breath in. What do you smell?"

"Cherry bark and almonds," he answered immediately.

"Hmm ... that's interesting. I've never heard the scent of the tropics or ocean described that way before."

"I wasn't describing either of those. That scent is you, and it's invading my senses right now." He cleared his throat.

"Oh, sorry, it must be the sunblock."

It's your shampoo, he almost corrected. He could smell it whenever she was near, and it drove him crazy. Like an addict, he inhaled again.

"Good," she said, praising the deep breath he took. "Now tell me, what do you feel?"

You. Her nearness surrounded him. *I want to ride that gorgeous body of yours until you can't sit anymore.* Aloud, he replied lamely, "I don't know."

"Is your heart pounding? Can you feel the rush from being this close? You have goose bumps."

"Yes, all those things," he acknowledged.

"Then you'll need to recall all of these feelings when you go to write about your visit."

Considering that's how he often felt when near Eve, that wouldn't be a problem. "But who cares how I feel?"

"The reader does. They may never get to be in your shoes, so they need to live vicariously through your words."

"I feel ... humbled."

"That's perfect. By nature? From feeling so powerless at this impressive height?"

"I feel humbled by *you*," Adam said, turning his head toward her and slowly opening his eyes to take her in. "You're remarkable."

She started when she turned and noticed his attention was on her. Stepping away, she looked around. Their quiet cocoon disappeared. "I ... I'm glad you're finally realizing it."

"I knew it immediately."

"Bullshit," Eve said with an exaggerated roll of her eyes. "You thought I wrote fluff. You teased me about being stuck on obits, and then you made it a point to tell me all the political contacts you knew and historic events that the great Adam Seager covered."

Jabbing a thumb at his chest, he asked in shock, "I did? I guess I was simply trying to impress you and have you notice me back."

She snorted. "How could anyone not notice you?"

That announcement had him smirking, but still, he wasn't sure if she meant it as praise or not.

"Well, it certainly came off as if ... as if you thought we were all beneath you."

He paused, taking in her words. "You're partially right there. I often think of *you* beneath me, more often than is healthy, but I have always had the greatest respect for your talent and ambition."

"Ha! Even when I was writing boring obituaries?"

"Yes, but they were never boring. You have the ability to bring these unknown people to life—even in death."

She shot him a disbelieving glare.

"I'm serious. You never once did a traditional obituary where so and so was married, had three kids, worked here, and lived there. You always included personal anecdotes. Like that woman who donated over fifty pints of blood over the course of her lifetime and was now donating her organs after she passed. Or that time you wrote about the retired cop who never left the state of Florida, but through his daily county patrols had probably driven the equivalent of around the world."

She gaped at him. "I ... uh ... I can't believe you remembered those details."

"Come on, I always made it a point to go by your desk and recite a line or two back to you."

"But ... but I thought you were mocking me, not praising me."

He sighed. Somehow, he'd really fucked up if that's what she thought. "Well, I do like teasing you, but not about that. When my father died, I was only fourteen, and I still remember how disappointed I was with his obituary. The paper listed the wrong birthdate, and there weren't any real details that spoke to the amazing man whom I knew. It bugged me so much that I actually called up the newsroom. They passed the buck and said they simply include what the funeral home gives them. I then chewed out the funeral director for not running it past us first. I like to think it was an early lesson on checking your sources and digging deeper."

Her big, blue eyes were glistening as they stared up at him. "I'm sorry, Adam," she said, placing a hand on his shoulder. "That really sucks that they did such a shoddy job. And I'm sorry your dad died when you were still so young."

He bobbed his head but didn't flee from the contact or the increasingly profound moment like he normally would have. He'd never shared that story before with anyone, but he was glad he did. That Eve knew this about him. The loss had definitely shaped him.

"I appreciate you telling me that. Not about my writing, but your experience. For opening up. I know that's not easy for you."

"You make it easy," he said, leaning in. He wasn't sure what the hell he was doing, only that he needed to be closer to her comforting smile that was drawing him stronger than the ocean's pull below.

"Did you just call Eve easy?" Hugh asked with a cold laugh, placing a palm on both of their backs, abruptly ruining his descent and bringing him back to the present moment.

"*Hugh* got to be kidding me," Adam said with all the annoyance he felt at the intrusion.

"Are we still doing that?" Hugh responded haughtily, slipping off his expensive sunglasses and hooking them into the opening of his shirt.

"*Hugh* aren't, but *we* are," Adam goaded. One step left and just maybe Hugh would fall off the cliff.

As if reading his thoughts, Hugh inched away from them. "I asked the divers to give us some tips for diving from the lower platform. I didn't bring a bather, but I suggested the American would be game. Fancy a dare?"

Adam glanced down to where Hugh pointed. The so-called lower ledge was still easily a thirty-foot drop. He shrugged. "No problem." He'd have jumped it anyway just to cool down, but now he had to do it for America and to shut the weasel up.

"Are you sure?" Eve asked, her brows knitted with concern. "Besides the jagged rocks, the water looks awfully choppy. We don't even know how deep it is."

"Eve, darling," Hugh patronized, "those guys do it dozens of times a day. They wouldn't if it wasn't safe. I'm sure your strong chap here can handle it."

"But they are professionals," Eve replied, eyeing the precipice.

Adam rested his hand on the small of Eve's back. "Not to worry, I got this." He pulled his T-shirt over his head, glad to be rid of it, and handed it to her. "Thanks," he added as she took it and stuffed it into her off-the-shoulder sack. Her eyes trailed over his bare chest. Good—turnabout was fair play. Although her hungry, hooded look as she focused on his tats and the way she unconsciously licked her lips had him wishing he could dive into her and not the ocean.

He should have reassured her with the knowledge that he competed as a diver in college, but he was eager to surprise her. Granted that was over a decade ago, but he relished knowing he could pull off a dive with some flair. He might not do it every day like these native divers did for tips, but he could manage at least one rotation from that height.

He spoke briefly with one of the divers in the conversational Spanish that he knew, letting them know he wasn't a novice. "¡Buena suerte!" the man said, giving him a thumbs-up with his well wishes.

Adam's pulse raced as he inhaled the salty spray of the ocean. Stepping toward the platform's edge, he took the proper stance, eyeballing the waters below to estimate the necessary angle he'd need to hit. Diving reminded him of a game of billiards, since both came down to physics, technique, and practice. The moment he sprang into the air, he knew he'd hit his mark. Still, the impact was harder than he expected, and the temperature much colder, too.

As he surfaced, he heard clapping and shouts. Eve seemed to be his biggest cheerleader. His gaze zeroed in on her wide eyes, and he called up to her, "Join me. It's refreshing!"

She froze mid-clap, then crossed her arms across her chest in a protective gesture. "No, thank you. I have nothing to prove."

"Come on, baby cakes, it would make for a fun story," he teased, treading water. "Or are you chicken?"

"Mature, very mature."

"Forget it," Hugh called down. "When Eve says no, she can be quite pigheaded about it."

"So, I'm a chicken *and* a pig?" she asked with a huff, flinging off her razorback tank top and slinking out of her form-fitting pants, revealing a barely there, black bikini. Thank goodness he was already in cold water because the sight of Eve in just the skimpy two-piece was making him hotter than ever. "Fine, I'll jump, and I'll have less of a splash, too," she boasted.

He couldn't help but chuckle as she marched defiantly to the jump point.

"You better move out of the way," she shouted down, losing some of her original bravado. Obediently, he scissor-kicked to the side. Eve made a motion as if she were about to leap but stalled mid-action. Pivoting, she took a step back. She shook her head before coming back to the edge and looking down once again. It was high, no doubt about that.

"Just take one small step forward and bring your arms and legs together like a pencil. Gravity will take care of the rest," he encouraged. "You can do it, and I'm here if you need me."

She nodded with conviction, and he knew this time, she wouldn't back away. Her eyes were focused, her face determined, and he already wanted to applaud her.

Following his directions, she took a measured step forward and descended to the water like a pro. True to her word, her splash was minimal, but several seconds after she'd entered the water, she still hadn't resurfaced. Adam scanned the water in search of her. Numerous, nerve-racking seconds went by, but still no Eve.

His heart pounding, Adam dived under the water. Spotting her as she swam upward, he reached out under the water, ready to tug her up if need be. They surfaced together, gasping for air.

"Are you okay?" he asked, his gaze roaming her face. He didn't spot any cuts.

Still, she shook her head frantically and shoved out of his hold. "Let me go," she demanded, eyes wide, before diving back under the water.

"What's wrong?" he asked the minute she bobbed her head back up again just to chin level, her shoulders and the rest of her body under the water.

"I lost my top!" she spit out from behind gritted teeth.

He howled with laughter and she splashed him, slinging saltwater into his open mouth. "It's not funny!"

"Oh, I beg to differ."

"Are you going to stand there and not help me?"

"I'm not standing anywhere, I'm swimming."

Her scowl revealed what she thought of his smart-ass correction. He considered the situation for a moment as he fought back his laughter. The ungentlemanly side of him very much wanted to dip underneath the lapping waters to see if she was telling the truth about her missing bikini top, but then he heard Hugh and some of the others inquiring from above. As much as he desperately wanted to see her naked body, he didn't want it to be under these circumstances, and he sure as hell didn't want anyone else to see her.

Speaking in Spanish again, he called up to their guide, requesting that he throw down his T-shirt from Eve's knapsack. The man helpfully did as instructed, much to the confusion of everyone observing them. The tee floated down near Adam and he immediately handed it to Eve.

"Thank you," she said, her eyes reflecting her gratitude. She swiftly put the shirt on, slipping under the water for a second.

"Come on, there's a ladder over there." He swam over to the rusty, I-hope-you-got-your-tetanus-shot metal structure that was somehow built into the cliff. He let her go first, figuring he'd be behind her if she fell, just in case.

"I guess I owe you once again?" she grumbled as they climbed the slippery rungs.

"Guess so," he replied, biting back the huge smile he wanted to emit. "But considering that's a white shirt, maybe we can call this one even."

With a gasp, Eve clutched the shirt to her chest with one hand. Her foot missing its intended step. He reached up to steady her, his hand inappropriately shoving her butt up higher so she could get back to the right spot. She grunted her thanks, and this time he didn't bother to hide his ear-to-ear beam.

When they reached the top, Eve gathered her own clothes and scampered off into the brush, his laughter following her.

Would she include this part of their adventure in her

recap? *Dear reader, when jumping off a cliff, remember not to wear a bikini.* If Eve didn't, he'd have to work it into his draft, if only to witness her making Nik remove it from the final. The idea had him laughing harder.

But first, he had an opportunity to goad her once again. "Oh honey bee," he called out to her, making sure his voice carried past the cluster of palm trees and plants she hid behind. "Can I pretty please have my shirt back? You know I'm not as flagrantly immodest as you are."

Her response came in the form of a wadded wet t-shirt being hurled at his face. She had good aim. Despite struggling to pull the soaked shirt back on, he smiled, he had good aim too and he was aiming for Eve with a Cupid's arrow.

17

After their adventure-filled morning with the group, Eve was looking forward to just chilling on board that afternoon as they set sail for the next port. Apparently, she wasn't alone. As she walked outside on the circular, teak deck with her beach bag slung over her shoulder, she spotted Adam by the mid-ship pool.

He was sprawled out on a lounge chair, which overlooked the pool, bar, and hot tubs, with the ocean and departing land at his back, just a head swivel away from view. He wore bright-orange swim trunks, aviator sunglasses, and nothing else. Despite the sunshade overhead, he was mostly in the sun. He'd apparently just gone for a swim, too, because beads of water still clung to his defined chest and rolled down his broad shoulders. His wet, jet-black hair was extra shiny as a result, with hints of blue like a raven's slick coat. He looked delectable with his muscular tanned legs stretched leisurely out in front of him. Still staring, she observed that he had nice feet for a man, large but smooth with a high arch.

Empty loungers sat on both sides of him, followed by a

towel pick-up station with a pyramid of rolled towels. Unnoticed still, she stood there debating if she should slink away to one of the other five pools on the ship or woman up and join him already. Their morning together had been a whirlwind of her trying to set up boundaries and him effectively breaking them down with an inviting touch, heated look, private moments, or a jump off a cliff. Her heart still soared from his praise in regard to her work. And this time, she accepted them as real. She'd been wrong in brushing them off before as teasing. Perhaps, in her fear of being hurt again, she'd assumed wrong and projected Hugh's critical nature on him. The realization was like a weight being lifted off her shoulders.

His gaze shifted toward her, his smoky eyes locking with hers. His unabashed smile made her mind up for her. She moved forward as if being pulled by an imaginary lasso that was all Adam.

"If it's not the woman with a thousand smiles," he said as she came closer, and she couldn't help but smile brighter.

She set her bag down on the empty chair to his left and grabbed one of the blue-and-white striped towels provided by the cruise line. "I thought you said I had a hundred smiles."

Adam shrugged. "The more time I spend with you, the more they add up," he said, folding his hands behind his head as if he hadn't a care in the world. Her eyes feasted on his biceps, and an image of her laying her head on them as he spooned her flitted into her mind. "Couldn't get enough of me, sweets, so you had to come find me?"

She groaned, the enticing image evaporating. Pivoting on her flip-flops she turned to leave, but he lunged forward and grabbed her elbow to stop her. "Sorry, old habits die hard. Please stay."

She reached for another towel and threw it at his face. "Here, you're dripping wet."

His smile turned wolfish as he scrubbed his hair dry. "I like dripping wet," he murmured, casting her a sexy wink.

She willed herself not to react to his teasing, especially when she'd accidentally thrown him such a softball to twist her words with. Instead, she concentrated on laying out her towel and digging out her sunblock and shades from her tote.

He eyed her metallic gold, halter swimsuit that she'd impulsively purchased on Amazon just for this trip. Luckily, the affordable buy fit her well and she didn't have to return it after all. From the way Adam's gaze lingered appreciatively, she should buy one in every color.

"I just played a game of pool volleyball, but I'll jump back in the water, goldie, if you'd like some company," he offered.

"No, thanks. I already showered when we got back, and my hair is finally dry." She sprayed her legs with the cool mist of sunscreen. "I just wanted some air before dinner and to take in the pool scene."

"And you found me doing the same," he added, adjusting his sunglasses. "Would you like me to get your back?" His head motioned toward the bottle in her hand.

She had packed a spray version of sunscreen that she could easily apply herself, but his help would offer more protection she reasoned, and all right, she itched to have his strong hands rub her down. "Fine, but no funny business," she warned, handing him the cannister.

"Funny business?" Her rebuke had him cracking up, shaking his head in mirth. Drops of water flung from his silky hair in the process.

It wasn't the first time he'd goaded her regarding the old-fashioned expressions she was prone to say. Not too surprising since she lived in a resort town where the median age was sixty-five. But truth be told, even before she moved to Naples, she'd been an old soul. "I almost said shenanigans," she admitted, laughing, too.

"Turn around," he ordered with a twirl of his trigger finger. She complied, sweeping her hair over one shoulder and sitting on her lounge chair with her legs cast over one side and her back to him. She was rewarded by hearing his sudden intake of breath. She'd almost forgotten that her cut on this bathing suit was very low, stopping at the dimples on her backside.

After a brief pause, he sprayed the sunscreen into his hands to absorb the initial cold impact. Thoughtful, but unnecessary, since she was already burning up imagining those strong, now-glistening hands massaging her.

His warm touch and the scent of coconut and exotic fruits filled her senses, more intoxicating than any tropical drink. It wasn't the coolness of the sunscreen that caused goose bumps to break out all over Eve's skin. Her whole body felt on fire as Adam's hands glided across her skin and under the straps of her bathing suit, gently massaging the nape of her neck. She sucked in her lip to keep from shivering, but unable to prevent bringing her shoulder up to her ear in reaction.

"Too hard?" he whispered.

Her heart pounded and she shook her head. "I like hard," she somehow managed to reply, and his slight chuckle came out more like a growl. The heat only increased as his hand slid lower and lower, skimming his fingers under the trim of her suit along her shoulder blades.

This is your coworker. You don't like him. It won't work. Eve repeated the phrases over and over as her body ignored each reminder.

"Define 'funny business.'" Adam's voice had deepened and sounded breathless. He didn't wait for her to respond before continuing. "So, I guess I shouldn't let my hands sweep under the sides of your bathing suit and come around to cup your beautiful breasts?"

"Uh ..." She literally had no intelligent words. The inappropriate image he presented sounded divine, her nipples hardening just thinking about it.

Adam jerked his hands away and stood abruptly. "All set, but thanks to your sunscreen, I'm desperately craving a piña colada right now with the strongest rum floater they have," he said roughly, taking a step toward the crowded bar. "Can I get you something?" he asked without turning around to look back at her, which she was grateful for. She didn't want him seeing the lust in her eyes.

"No," Eve finally breathed out, and he nodded, leaving her to stare at his retreating butt like it was the last lifejacket in a shipwreck.

She should have chosen another pool. She was in way over her head, and she hadn't even entered the water.

18

Another scheduled dinner sitting next to Eve, their arms brushing. At least Adam was allowed to stare at his leisure, acting the besotted fool that he really was. Although, technically, he didn't have to, since Hugh hadn't joined their group again this evening. Several others had made their excuses as well, claiming today's shore excursion had worn them out. They had all started their day cave tubing, followed by sight-seeing and a little market shopping in Belize.

Adam, on the other hand, was far from tired. Ready to jump out of his skin was more like it. He couldn't take another night brooding alone, knowing Eve was lying in the bed only feet away. The bartender on deck six knew him by name at this point and greeted him each evening like he was the mayor of the darkened sports bar. This was followed by waking up unfulfilled and running off his steam in the gym. Then repeat.

Time to mix things up. Nothing was going to change if he didn't take another tack. He and Eve needed some quality time together, just the two of them, and outside their stifling room.

After the meal, he held out her chair and exited the dining room alongside her, but he blocked her path to the stairs. "Come on, slim, don't go to bed just yet." Before she even made a move, he sensed that she was about to shake her head no, so he pushed further. "At least make a proper man out of me and buy me a drink. You know, take me out on the town, or ... around the deck, I guess."

A smile tugged on her lips. "It's been a long day," she drawled out, sounding unsure.

He could feel victory in sight, though. It was time to play one of his cards. "You owe me, doll face."

"Fine, but can you cool it on the pet names? Hugh isn't here."

Thank goodness for that. He intended to make sure she remembered that fact tonight. "No promises, Richards. You are on my terms."

He hooked his arm with hers and pulled slightly in the direction of the main piazza. She laughed and followed in step with him, which was impressive given the strappy high heels she had on. At work, she usually wore flats and functional, albeit flattering—and always colorful—work attire. The new, dazzling fashion she donned each day on their vacation had him enthralled. Tonight's backless, red dress was no exception.

"Where to, master?" Eve asked with a sarcastic huff as they stood under the rotunda.

He almost tripped over his own feet. "Please do feel free to use *that* pet name for me as much as you want. Wear it out, say it louder so everyone can hear. Honestly, I don't mind."

Her throaty laugh had him breaking out in chills. He

must be a masochist. "Let's have some fun in the casino," he suggested.

She lifted one shoulder in indifference. "Yes, master."

He didn't bother controlling his resulting growl as he moved faster to usher her in the direction of the gaming area.

The mood was instantly exciting and enticing. The stark difference from the tranquil hallway to the loud and flashy casino was jarring for the first couple of seconds. Sensory overload. Not too dissimilar to the sensations he experienced when he would first gaze upon Eve each morning at work.

Inside the casino, the ceiling lights were muted, allowing the glow of hundreds of slot machines to fill the room. A catchy, upbeat song blasted from hidden speakers, and the thrilling sounds of gambling drew them in. Unfortunately, the casino wasn't a smoke-free area on the ship, but luckily, not many were partaking, or at least the stench wasn't overpowering.

"Pop quiz. What won't you find in a casino?" he asked.

"A winner?" she joked. "A clock and windows. Everyone knows that."

Clearly, she wasn't impressed with his gambling-world knowledge. "Okay, smarty pants, shall we find some side-by-side slot machines?" He headed to a row of shiny, high-tech-looking ones.

Eve halted. "Slots? They have the worst odds in the house. Maybe I should get your cane, too, grandpa?"

He bit his cheek to stop from laughing at her sassiness. "All right, ace, let's take it up a notch then. How about blackjack?"

"Hmm," she murmured, scanning the room. "I like you,

Adam, I really do, but I hate when someone hits when they aren't supposed to and ruins my hand."

He choked on his laugh. "Are you implying I don't know how to properly play the game?" The idea would rankle if he wasn't delighted by her cockiness. He'd spent many late nights playing cards and gambling with the troop members he'd been stationed with over the years. It was both a stress reliever and an easy way to bond.

Pursing her lips, she gave him a long once-over that had him straightening under her scrutiny. "I'm sure you can play ..." She trailed off as if measuring him along with her precise words. "But I bet you're the type to go all in even when the odds are against you."

She had that right. He couldn't help pointing his finger like a gun and aiming it at her. He just hoped it looked playful and not corny. "I'll take that for the compliment it wasn't intended to be." That had her eyebrows rising. "And consider yourself warned—I do plan on going all in."

She flipped her golden hair over her shoulder and strode toward the back of the casino where people were crowded around the gaming tables. "Alrighty, what's left?" he asked, following her like a puppy. "Roulette?"

"I like the game," she said, throwing him a glance over her shoulder, "but you can lose your shirt too quickly."

"Oh, then we should definitely play that!" He tugged at her dress, slowing her stride so they were side by side once again. "Especially if the same can be said for losing hot, li'l red dresses."

"Hmm ... looks like there already is a Texas Hold'em tournament going on," she continued, ignoring what he thought was a rather clever barb.

He tried again. "There's always strip poker."

"I doubt that's a casino-approved game."

"It should be," he grumbled, scanning the different tables. "I can teach you how to play craps," he offered. "It has a low house advantage."

Her hands immediately came up to rest on her hips. "Um ... chauvinist much?" She evidently read the lost expression on his face. "I already know how to play craps, thank you very much. I grew up going to Atlantic City with my mom and her high-rolling boyfriend. In college, I spent each spring break in Vegas. My friends called me Hard Eight."

"Well, damn." How was it possible she just got hotter? His eyes almost bugged out of his head as she proceeded to order two shots of whiskey from the passing server and then informed the man that they'd be over at the far craps table. Was this seriously the same perky princess of the *Tribune* newsroom?

Her resulting peal of laughter ran through him, almost causing him to collapse at her cute little feet and kiss his way up her sexy legs. But if he kept thinking along those lines, "Hard Eight" was going to be his nickname, too. As it was, he had to check the impulse to rearrange himself.

"My apologizes. Okay, hot shot, why don't you show me what you got," he said, brandishing his hand with a flourish so she would lead the way. He gladly followed yet again.

They exchanged their key cards with the pit boss for chips, each pulling one hundred in ten pieces. They took their spots among a group of four guys. Given their proprietary and relaxed stances, they'd been playing for some time already. All nodded in greeting, and the man to Eve's left moved over to give her extra space to settle in. He also waved his hand to skip his turn in favor of letting her be the next roller.

"New shooter," called the stickman, passing Eve several

new red die to select from. With one hand, she grabbed the two in the middle while the others were removed. "Place your bets!"

Adam preferred not to roll. You could concentrate and play the board more without having to be bothered throwing the dice, too. He'd once rolled for a good half hour yet made less than everyone else who'd won big off his luck. Normally, he also liked to sit back and watch everyone for a little bit before participating, taking everything in, then going all in as Eve surmised.

He placed his bets on the Pass line, and Eve bobbed her head in acknowledgement, then doubled down on the Pass line as well. He wasn't dumb enough to bet against her, even if he did lose all his money. It wasn't good protocol to bet against friends, never mind ones you wanted to sleep with.

Lady Luck incarnate jiggled the cubes for a second in her hand before expertly tossing them to the back wall.

"Eleven. Pass line wins."

The employees cleared the bets for those who bet on the Don't Pass line and paid out everyone else. Adam let his chips ride, and Eve gave him a smirk. Damn but he wanted to kiss her right there at the table. For luck, obviously.

Her next roll placed the puck on the number nine, and the older man at the end of the table groaned, evidently not happy with the odd number. Everyone else scrambled to place new bets. Eve kept her bet on the Pass line and added bets to the eight and Hard Eight, staying true to her lucky numbers. Adam threw down a chip on the Come line, sparking a raised eyebrow from her.

He leaned in and murmured, "Good luck" in her ear before she picked up the dice to shoot again.

"Oh, I'm going to make it rain," she sang, motioning her fingers to mimic rain falling down. Her effort to be baller only accomplished the opposite, and he had to bite back his hoot of laughter.

"Oh, really? Care to make it interesting?" he baited.

She turned to him, her eyes flashing with excitement. "What did you have in mind?"

"I have a lot of things on my mind, beautiful, especially when it comes to you, but I'd settle for you spending another hour up past bedtime with me."

"What are the terms?"

"I bet you'll crap out before you roll one of your Hard Eights, or even an easy eight."

"Deal! Wait, but what do I get?"

"Name it," he said, waggling his eyebrows. *Please say a night of wild sex. Please say a night of wild sex.*

"My debts with you cleared."

Oomph. "Fine," he agreed.

"Shooter?" the stickman yelled, bringing Eve back to the game. She did the same jiggle and toss, the dice bouncing off the padded back wall with ease.

"Ten," the stickman called and paid the anti-nine man.

"You lived to do another roll, but still not what you needed," Adam taunted.

Eve huffed and reached for the dice with a look of extreme focus on her face. *So hot.* He had to force his eyes away from her face to see the outcome of her roll.

"Ten again."

"Don't even say it," she muttered under her breath, already reaching for the dice.

"I wouldn't dream of it, Hard Eight," he baited, not letting her get the last word.

Next was a five. She was making some of the players richer, but neither of them. Finally, she rolled an unlucky seven.

"Craps!" shouted the stickman, causing several to cheer and others to boo.

Adam had lost forty bucks, but he'd won their bet.

The stickman cleared the table and motioned to pass the dice to Adam. He shook his head and stopped Eve from placing any new bets. "Oh no you don't. I'm not wasting our extra hour here." The waiter from earlier took that moment to arrive with their shots of whiskey. "Why don't we bring these over to the bar," he suggested, grabbing their drinks before she could answer.

It was his lucky night after all. The horseshoe-shaped bar was empty, and he couldn't have been happier.

"Shall we?" she asked, hoisting the tumbler up to her parted lips.

"Not yet." He stilled her arm and settled in on the barstool. She threw him a quizzical look. "Ever play the drinking game *Never Have I Ever*?"

There was his smile. Man, did she make him work for it tonight, which made it all the sweeter. "Not since college, drinking forties."

"The guys and I used to play during military leaves abroad. Fun way to get your buddies drunk, but it's also helpful to get to know one another, too."

"And which one is your angle tonight?" she asked, her scarlet dress hiking up as she hopped up on the high bar seat next to him, revealing the long line of her legs down to her strappy heels that dangled just above the brass-bar footrest.

"Both," he admitted with a smile of his own, admiring her. "Remember, you have to take a sip if the answer is yes. Since I won our last bet, I'll go first." He picked up his glass and held it aloft, and she followed suit. "Never have I ever dated a coworker."

"Cheap shot. You know I have," Eve whined.

"I don't make the rules, Richards. Drink," he urged.

She did, glaring at him as she sloshed back the amber liquid and then licked her lips. The action wasn't meant to be teasing, but hell if it didn't have him adjusting just the same.

"My turn," she said eagerly. "Never have I ever been on a cruise."

Yup, smart cookie indeed. He drank a big gulp and leaned closer, their elbows touching on the countertop. Notes of whiskey and the ever-present, cherry bark-and-almond scent that clung to her wafted over him. He inhaled, getting high on her alone. The resulting euphoria wasn't new. Her breathing him in, though, in return and the hinting gleam of sexual interest in her arousing stare was.

"Never have I ever been to all fifty states," he supplied, reaching automatically for his glass, but she did not.

"You've been to all fifty states?" she questioned, looking skeptical.

"You're not the only one with wanderlust," he replied with a shrug. "Only my wandering has been domestic-based. I took a year off before college, living out of my car, writing about the people I met along the way and seeking out small-town charm."

"Is that why you settled in little Old Naples?"

He made a buzzer sound. "Sorry, that wasn't in a *Never Have I Ever* question format." Her blue eyes flared, and he found himself grinning at her short-lived flash of anger. "What states are you missing?"

"Hmm." She scrunched up her nose as she counted to herself before listing them out. "Wisconsin, the Dakotas, Alaska, and West Virginia."

"Not too bad. We'll have to work on kicking those out for you."

Her eyebrow lifted at his use of *we*.

"Maybe pitch an Alaskan cruise next," he rushed out, plowing through the temporary awkwardness.

"As long as you're my guide," she said quietly, and his pulse raced at her invitation. He didn't have a chance to dwell on the feeling, though, before she started the game up again. "Uh ... never have I ever smoked cigarettes."

He grumbled and reached for his drink. "Just socially here and there when I was younger," he explained after his swallow. "Never have I ever gotten a tattoo," he supplied, throwing her a softball and taking another drink in admission to his arm bands. He almost choked when he saw that she did the same. "You have a tattoo?" He'd seen a lot of her already, so where the hell was this tat?

"Also something I did on spring break in Vegas," she admitted, clearly pleased with herself for surprising him. "And my parents still bring it up."

"I bet," he said absently. "Are you going to share what it's of, or better, where it is?"

"Nope."

"You're cruel," he said, shooting back his entire drink even though he wasn't supposed to. Bad enough he was dying to see her naked, but now he desperately had to discover this tattoo. "If it says *Hugh*, I'll pay for your tattoo removal," he grumbled.

She chuckled and shot back her drink, too, with only the slightest grimace evident, then smacked the empty glass on the counter. He wanted to lick her glistening lips and envied the back of her hand when it wiped across the moistened flesh. "I didn't even know him then," she said with an amused shake of her head.

"Is it any guy's name?" he asked, hating himself for sounding jealous. It was unreasonable, but he breathed easier when she shook her head again. His relief turned playful. "A girl's name?"

Her laughter was contagious. Sliding his keycard over, he signaled for the waiter to give them another round. Not only did he want to get to know Eve better by playing this silly game, but it was also his chance to prove himself, too. "Never have I ever cheated on my partner," he stated.

Neither made a motion to grab for their drink, which was also a good thing since they hadn't been refilled yet anyway.

"Never have I ever had my heart broken," she supplied.

Their drinks arrived just in time for them both to take a sip.

"How long ago?" she asked, and he tsked at her follow-up question. "Come on," she urged, "I supplied a little more with your tattoo curiosity."

She had a point. "Her name was Kelly," he answered. "A rising political lobbyist who had no interest in leaving D.C." She'd broken up with him as soon as she heard about his plans, a whole month before he'd even left. He shrugged. It was all for the best, considering he'd had a lot on his mind then and it wouldn't have worked out long term. How could it, given his situation?

"She chose a state over you?" she asked, sounding aghast yet also playful while repeating almost what he had said about her and Hugh.

He raised his arms in a what-can-I-say gesture and racked his brain for a more lighthearted question. "Never have I ever gone skinny dipping."

They both sipped, and again he was impressed by her adventurous nature.

"Never have I ever had sex in a public place," she stated with a waggle of her brows.

"Prove it," he urged after seeing her drink, confirming that alcohol had indeed made him bolder and drained what little willpower he had left because he was definitely picturing the possibility in delicious detail.

She let out a sexy laugh and looked around the room. "Here?"

"Anywhere," he dared.

She laughed and swatted at his arm.

"Never have I ever had sex on a cruise ship," he amended. Neither drank, and her blue eyes fixed on his. "Lord, would I love to change that," he added, his voice husky. Unable to stop himself, he lightly ran his fingers up and down her bare arm, her wide eyes following his movements, softening as he continued his trail. "While I've never dated a coworker or experienced the fallout, I'm not Hugh," he said solemnly.

"I know that," she said primly, sitting straighter in her stool.

"Do you?" he asked, cupping her chin so she would look at him. "I swear I'd never screw you over professionally ... just, you know, in the bedroom," he teased, before sobering his tone again and gently reaching his other hand up to cradle her face in his rough hands. "Eve, I'm not a player, and I'm old enough to know what I want, and frankly, I want you. Not just sexually, although yes, boy do I want to fuck your brains out. But I also want things that I haven't wanted in a very long time."

"Like what?" she asked on a breathy whisper, her wide eyes staring into his soul.

"I want to see your beautiful smile outside of work. Take you out on a date. You can pick the place, too, since you know all the fun spots. Whatever you want to do, I'm game. Mini golf, done. Dancing again? I'd love to. Brunch? You got it. A walk on the beach? For sure. Yoga? I don't think I can pull it off without getting a hernia, but I'd try. I'll embarrass myself at Karaoke even. I'm willing to try a lot with you, if you'd let me."

She looked stunned, not uttering a word for what seemed like the longest seconds of his life, but he could feel her pulse racing beneath his fingertips as he gently caressed her neck and jaw. The tense moments reminded him of the eerie, in-between time after hearing the whistle of a rocket-propelled grenade and not knowing where it was going to detonate. Not knowing if it was your lucky day or your last day. The fleeting thoughts of everything you ever loved and would miss as you took cover. When seconds felt like hours.

"And you thought you couldn't write flowery or share your opinion?" she finally said, turning her head slightly to lay a kiss on his nearby hand. It was sweet as hell, and the affectionate gesture tugged at his heart further. "Why don't we start with a stroll on the upper deck," she suggested. "I doubt that will be hernia-inducing."

Adam signed the bill for their drinks as soon as the bartender placed the slip down, practically ripping it from his hands. He left one of his remaining ten-dollar chips as a tip to make up for his eagerness to get the hell out of there. He did not want to waste a moment with Eve.

19

Eve stared in wonder at their intertwined hands, which swung slightly as they walked companionly in sync on the upper deck. Their arms needlessly grazed, just because they could. She craved the contact and was enjoying how the raised hair on his arms brushed hers. She wrestled back the urge to fight her workplace misgivings. It felt too right to be wrong. Jada *had* said Eve shouldn't overthink it and just have fun, but she sensed this could be more —much more.

Granted, she was slightly tipsy from the whiskey, but that wasn't why her head was spinning. That was due to the giddiness she felt inside from his confession that he wanted to date her. No, her mind was clear when it came to Adam, and her heart swelled with joy with each step they took together.

Letting go of his hand, she walked toward the teak railing, allowing the gentle ocean breeze wrap around her a second before Adam did the same. His solid arms hugged her from behind, placing her body up against his broad chest. She let out an audible sigh of contentment as she breathed in his spicy, cedarwood scent. Leaning down, he brushed a soft kiss across her cheek, sending delicious chills through her body.

They stayed joined like that for a few moments, staring out at the dark ocean in each other's embrace. The moonlight floated down like a spotlight just for them. Neither were in a hurry to talk as they enjoyed the connection. The unspoken was just as strong, as if they'd confessed all their thoughts. After all her travels, she finally felt like she was home in his arms. For the first time, she felt completely comfortable knowing there was nowhere else she'd rather be or no one else she'd rather be with.

All right, that wasn't entirely true. She bit back a smirk. There was somewhere else she'd rather they were right now. Turning around, she buried her face into his neck, sucking and licking along the way. His hot skin tasted a little salty, like the air around them. "Let's go back to our room," she whispered near his collarbone. Proudly saying *our* sent a possessive thrill through her.

He cleared his throat, and she felt the vibration under her lips. "If we go back to the cabin together, you know what's going to happen, right?"

God, she hoped so. Still, her nerves were dancing with all the uncertainties. "Yes, but I don't do one-night stands," she said, trying her best to come off more confident than she felt at the moment.

He placed his hands on her shoulders and tipped her back so she could look up at him with ease. "Good, because I'm not looking to hit it and quit it," he joked, before intensity darkened his eyes. "When it comes to you, there's so much I want to do—too much to pack into one night, Eve."

"Well, we have three nights left on board," she supplied.

He shook his head. "I'm going to need longer than that."

Her heart leapt into her throat. He was telling her everything she wanted to hear. She just hoped he meant it. None of this fuckboy ghosting shit that was so prevalent with guys today, but then again, that was the gamble you took with any new start. Adam wasn't a boy, though. He was a man who knew what he wanted, and he seemed to want her. He was sincere and loyal—she'd known that even before this trip. It was one of the first commendable things she'd observed outside of his playful bantering.

She pushed off the railing. Tugging on his arm, she tossed him a smile over her shoulder and led him to the stairwell toward their cabin.

When they reached their door, he pulled her to a stop. "Let me," he said, slipping the room key from his blazer's pocket. He stuck his foot in the doorway to keep it propped open but did not enter. Before she could ask what the holdup was, he lunged forward, scooping her up from behind her knees and shoulders. Cradling her into his arms, he carried her over the threshold. A giggle lodged in her throat at his spontaneous and romantic gesture. Gently, he released her, sliding her body down the length of him and gathering her back into a passionate kiss before her toes had yet to touch the floor.

"Now, as much as I love this dress, it needs to go," he growled. Her balance was thrown off when he abruptly let go of his hold, and she clung to his broad shoulders to right herself. "Strip," he commanded after she continued to hesitate.

"I will if you will," she dared.

"You're on," he said with a big smile, tossing his jacket immediately to the floor and unbuttoning his shirt. She was so transfixed by his movements, she forgot she wasn't holding up her part of the deal. Standing in front of him, she pulled her dress up and over her head in one swift movement.

She delighted in his gasp and the way he did a double take upon discovering she had nothing on underneath. Just the proud smile she wore now. His hands stilled at his belt buckle, but his eyes drank her in, roaming up and down with appreciation. It made her feel powerful, standing there stark naked before him. Watching him watch her had her core swiftly getting wetter, and they had just begun. Her pulse raced, knowing so much more was still to come.

"You're so fucking sexy," he said, starting to move and undress again. "I hope you know that. You literally took my breath away just now. Thank fuck I didn't know about your lack of bra and panties earlier because I don't think I would have lasted through dinner. No way could I have thought of anything else."

"Hmm," she drawled out, moving forward to run a finger down his bared chest. "So, I guess I shouldn't mention that the other day when I was perched on your desk at work, I didn't have on panties then, either."

He growled and she stood prouder, enjoying his lustful focus. "You're making it harder for me to get out of these pants." Despite his words, he managed to tug them and his boxers over his impressive erection, letting them fall to his feet. He deftly kicked the garments away, tugging his socks off with his toes in the process.

Boldly, Eve looked over his body. She wasn't done shocking him. She dropped to her knees in front of him, enjoying his groan as she settled between his thighs. Gripping her hands on his hips, she drew him an inch forward, digging her nails into his flesh. She trailed her tongue along his shaft, and he hissed as she planted a wet kiss at the base of his cock before slowly brushing her lips up the length of him in circular, teasing motions. Taking him into her mouth, she twirled her tongue around his velvety tip, then took him in deeper as she sucked. Bobbing her head up and down, she was just learning the taste of him when his hands fisted into her hair, but he didn't push her forward as she expected. Instead, he gently pulled her head away.

She gave him a petulant stare.

He shook his head in return. "There's plenty of time for that later. My turn to taste. I need you now up on that bed, baby girl."

"Oh, really? Is that so?" she mocked sternly. Well, as sternly as someone can sound when bare naked and on their knees. Not to mention how turned on she was from him calling her "baby girl." Still, she was irked that he sounded so confident and cocky about there being a later. Although, to be fair, she did just have his cock in her mouth, so he probably had every right to be both of those things. But dammit, she wasn't done being in control yet.

Before she could properly complain or take him back into her mouth, Adam abruptly pulled her upright and scooped her up into his arms, as if she weighed nothing at all. She clung to him with a gasp, even more turned on now. He threw her down on the middle of the bed causing her to flop and giggle from the unexpected impact.

Circling her ankles with his big hands, he tugged her closer to where he apparently wanted her to be while spreading her wider in the process. Her desire flared as she looked into his hooded eyes, which were focused on her exposed pussy. She could feel herself getting wetter just from his prolonged stare, like a heat lamp trained on her flesh. Although slightly embarrassed, she soon forgot that silly worry when his hands began to move. They lightly trailed up the inner length of her legs to her thighs, which he deliciously squeezed and kneaded, his firm grip splayed just below her opening.

Eve could only feel. The dizzying tangling of their tongues seemed to go on forever. How could she have forgotten how sexy kissing was? They both writhed on the bed as a result. She never wanted to stop.

Intertwining their fingers, Adam moved one of their joined fists straight above her head, bringing her breasts closer to his bare chest. Their other entangled pair of hands he anchored just by her shoulder, pushing her into the bed and effectively locking her beneath his body. Instinctually, she bucked and tugged, testing his hold. It was firm and unyielding.

He chided her pathetic attempt and nipped below her ear. Soothing the playful bite with his tongue, he ran it farther toward the hollow at the base of her neck, drawing her skin into his mouth to suck on. The scrape of his slight stubble against her sensitive skin caused an additional shiver and sigh to run through her body.

She could feel his smile form against her collarbone as he continued to delve lower. She jolted when he brushed his full lips along her nipple, back and forth across her hardened nub. Quick flicks of his tongue against the stiffed buds teased and frustrated her, causing a moan of pleading to escape from her dry lips. She wanted to clutch the back of his head and fasten his warm mouth there, but dammit, she didn't have a free hand.

Instead, she squeezed their tangled fingers tighter, wiggled closer, and arched forward. When he rewarded her with exactly what she wanted, Eve let his cocky smile pass. He sucked her aching breast into his mouth and drew on her hard and deep, giving each yearning globe the same dedication.

But when he moved back up to her neck, she wanted to pinch him. "I thought you said you wanted a taste?"

"I'm getting there," he said, releasing her hands and moving downward to kiss her abdomen.

It wasn't low enough. "Then get there," she growled, and his rumble of laughter sparked a new tremor of lust through her. "Found it," he said, kissing the compass tattoo on her hip, flicking his tongue on each directional point. "I should have guessed."

"That wasn't where I was talking about," she muttered, and he trailed laughing kisses from her left hip toward her belly button. She normally hated her stomach touched, but he didn't seem to notice or care about her lack of abs. On the contrary, he placed reverent kisses and twirled his tongue before finally dragging it down her stomach to the top of her sex. His lengthy exhale tickled and reignited her core.

Slowly, he parted her folds with a languid, upward stroke of his tongue, causing her breath to become shallow as she dragged air into her lungs. He found and flicked her aching bud, teasing it mercilessly back and forth and up and down. She wiggled underneath him, both enjoying and being frustrated by his teasing when she needed more.

"Enough," she cried out, trying to move away from his delicious torture.

"Never enough," he growled back into her pussy.

"Please! Time for that later," she begged, repeating his plea from earlier.

Slowly, he brought his head and body up, placing his knees in between hers and their eyes locked. The moment was charged beyond just the expected sexual tension. It felt ... well, more.

"Evie, are you sure you want to do this? Because this isn't

part of some make-believe boyfriend role for me. I've wanted this—*you*—for a really long time. Hell, I might already be in love with you."

Her heart practically flipped. "Nothing about you is make-believe, Adam. I want you, too."

His tight muscles relaxed. "Thank God, because as high school as this might sound, I think I might die if I had to leave this cabin right now."

She smiled up at him, glad to see she wasn't the only one desperate. "I should have a condom in my makeup bag," she said, pointing to the leather, Coach-emblemed bag that lay on top of the vanity behind him.

"Just one?" he whined.

"You're lucky I have that one," she declared. "I definitely wasn't expecting this. Were you?"

"I *definitely* had hoped. Dreamed … imagined … prayed … you name it." Adam crossed the cabin and rifled through her bag, none too carefully. "Where in the hell—found it!"

In a flash, he'd ripped open the gold foil and sheathed himself. Rejoining her on the bed, he brought his face down to hers to capture her lips in another thought-obliterating kiss before thrusting forward.

Eve's eyes opened wide as he filled her. Her nipples immediately hardened, and she broke out in goose bumps as he entered her. She tilted her head back and swallowed a moan as he settled in deep. For a second or two, neither moved, beyond his labored breathing and rapid heartbeat, which seemed to drum directly into her own chest. Holy cow, did he feel amazing! She'd be happy with just this. Almost.

Rocking back, she feared for a second that he was going to withdraw from her completely, but he stopped just as the tip of him began to leave her wet warmth. Teasing them both, he kept it teetering there for a prolonged second before he rocked back into her, seemingly having all the time in the world. Which she supposed they did, but dammit, Eve wasn't in the mood to play or go slow. She was more than ready for the bliss she knew they could give each other. When he finally plunged forward again, she released her moan. He continued to frustrate the hell out of her as he repeated this languid lovemaking process over and over.

He had her hands gripped and held above her again. Otherwise, she'd be clutching and thrusting his hips forward ... deeper, rougher. Instead, she had to settle for wrapping her legs around him. She tried wiggling her hips, but still, it didn't seem to tempt his cool, steady rhythm. Thankfully, with each slide into her, he ground his pelvis against her clit, harder and harder, causing the pressure inside her to build.

"No, not yet," she pleaded. She hadn't even gotten a chance to tease him, to make him wild like he was doing to her. She would have been pissed if it hadn't felt so fucking good. Rotating his hips back and forth, he chuckled lightly. "Just a little one. Please, baby girl, cum on my cock for me."

Her body jerked in response. Oh, damn, his filthy words were making her wetter. She was a slave to every sensation. Tilting her head back again, she desperately sucked on whatever skin of his she could find within reach. With no self-control left, she let herself just feel where their bodies met and played. Her release wasn't a "little one." No, it had her screaming out and bucking frantically beneath him. His body stilled as she convulsed around him.

"Damn, I felt that," he groaned, burying his face in her neck while she caught her breath.

"You have to free my hands because I need to maul you."

"I like the sound of that," he said with a wolfish smile.

Releasing his grip, he flipped them and reversed their positions, still managing to never lose their intimate connection.

Seated on top of him, Eve shifted and slid down farther on his shaft. Adam's resulting groan came out more like a whimper. Good. No mercy. She reached a hand behind her and gently touched his balls, causing him to buck slightly. It was her turn to torment.

Leaning over him, she delighted in noticing how his skin broke out into goose bumps as she lightly trailed her breasts and nipples down his hard chest. After her second playful brush across his torso, Adam roped his arms tightly around her back, bringing her breasts firmly down onto him. They both moaned from her being pressed against him. Dammit.

Pushing back against his hold, she sat up straight, pressing him deep into her. He whimpered as if she was hurting him, instead of providing the pleasure she knew he felt. She continued to wiggle as she got into a more comfortable position, but his hands suddenly dug into her ass cheeks and propelled her forward, commanding that she ride him. It felt too good not to comply. She rocked back and forth, finding a fast-paced rhythm that had them both sighing and caressing each other frantically. Her own tension began building once again.

"God, you feel so good. Please, baby, will you cum for me one more time?" Adam asked through heavy breaths. His body bowed and sweat broke out across his chest, but Adam remained still, allowing Eve to use him to find her peak once again.

She picked up her pace and let her release be her answer as she fell apart around him, collapsing on top of his chest. Adam planted a quick kiss on her temple before finally moving rapidly inside her. She clenched her walls against him when she felt that he was close, both helping to aid him and so she could selfishly feel every twitch as he came. He groaned her name as he pumped into her and found his release.

Spent, they lay there breathing deeply for several minutes. Eventually, Adam shifted and adjusted their joined bodies so that they were spooning. Gently, he gathered her hair, moving away the strands that were hitting her face. He brushed kisses on her temple, forehead, and cheeks. "Wow," he finally said, his voice gravelly. "No wonder Adam took a bite of Eve's apple. I don't blame the poor dude one bit."

Laughing, she wiggled her butt against his groin and nuzzled in closer. "Yeah, yeah, all her fault, too."

"That's right," he confirmed, nipping at her shoulder. "Adam was a helpless victim, just like I've been, at your mercy ever since I laid eyes on you."

She smiled drowsily, bone tired and gloriously happy. It was a delicious combo if you asked her.

20

They'd picked the worst night to hook up, only getting two hours of sleep in between their lovemaking. When the 6:00 a.m. wake-up alarm went off, both of them were dazed. Blearily, they rushed to get ready, trampling on their discarded clothes from yesterday as the ship docked ashore in Jamaica.

This time, Eve didn't balk at Adam's suggestion to share a quick shower. They didn't have a second to spare. Still, he glided the bar of soap over her quivering body and whispered into her ear a sexy promise describing all the things he would do the next time they were naked and under running water. Yes, please!

She could barely keep her eyes open and her head from bobbing on their bus ride on uneven pavement to their first tour point. Seeing her failed attempts to stay awake, Adam wrapped his arm around her shoulder and gently placed her head on his shoulder. She managed to mutter a contented "thanks" before falling fast asleep on him.

She felt like a princess when Adam kissed her awake. She only hoped she hadn't been drooling and didn't resemble the witch in the fairy tale. Bewildered, she looked around to find the bus had stopped at their destination and that everyone was unloading. Unintended, she caught the gaze of Hugh at the front of the bus, who stood in the aisle glaring back at her until Pamela asked him to move.

"Ready, Sleeping Beauty?" Adam asked, grabbing both of their backpacks. The small, chivalrous gesture wasn't lost on her. In her many years of traveling, no one had helped carry her bags outside of a paid porter. And what, had he read her thoughts about the Disney dream?

She was awake yet living in a fantasy with Prince Charming. Hell, their first planned activity for the day was to go horseback riding on the beach. Adam was even given a white horse to ride. She had to pinch herself. Was it Adam or the whole situation that had her wanting to skip, sing to birds, and say the L word already?

She'd ridden before at petting zoos and dude ranches, but trotting on the horses into the brush and galloping along the white, sandy beach line with the turquoise waters sparkling alongside was out of this world. The best part was at the end when they went bareback on the horses and out into the water. It was a thrilling experience to try and hold on to the huge animal as it became weightless in the waves and followed the path they must now know by heart. Eve had no idea horses could swim and that they enjoyed it, all of which she needed to share with her readers.

"Can this get any more touristy?" a bored British voice asked from behind her as she handed the reins of Sparkles over to the staff.

She shook her head before turning to face Hugh. Nope, the frog was not going to ruin her mood or story this time.

"Isn't that who we're writing for? Tourists?" Adam chimed in as he joined them.

Hugh straightened. "You two might be writing for the lowest common denominator, but I'd like to think my readers are more highbrow than this." He threw up an irritated hand at poor Sparkles' retreating backside. The horse's glossy, brown tail swooshed, splashing sprinkles of water their way. Eve tried her hardest not to laugh as Hugh attacked the droplets on his face. It wasn't easy.

"I had an amazing time," Eve said cheerfully. "I'd even say it was a bucket-list adventure. I'm sorry to hear you didn't enjoy it."

"Well, I'm sorry, too," Hugh huffed and walked away, giving Sparkles a wide berth.

Eve sighed and shrugged, not wanting there to be such animosity between them, yet still too blessedly happy to let his mood bother her anymore.

"I loved it," Adam said, drawing Eve back to who was truly making her happy. It might be her fanciful thoughts, but his dark eyes seemed to be twinkling with joy, too. Leaning down to her ear, he whispered, "Although, between last night and today's ride, I'm hoping your thighs aren't too sore."

She snorted. "I'm sure there is some witty, stallion reference for me to make, but I'm too tired to come up with it."

"Then I must take you to bed at once," Adam said, playfully scooping her up and twirling her right there on the beach. She giggled and held on tight. Yes, she was surely in the pages of a fairy tale come to life.

He gave her a quick kiss that hinted at more before placing her back down on her feet and picking up her discarded flip-flops.

"This is insane," she murmured, not necessarily intending for her thoughts to have been spoken aloud.

"What is?" he asked, kneeling in front of her and slipping her sandals on to her sandy feet like a glass slipper.

"This! You. Us," she sputtered, giving him a swat on his arm as he stood, both for emphasis and so she could confirm he was real. One eyebrow shot up at her outburst. He didn't back away, stepped closer instead, crowding her with his salty, fresh scent and heat, causing her knees to almost buckle. "I mean, it's all so unbelievable and sudden."

"Is it?" he asked, dusting off some sand from her shoulder, his finger circling the dark freckle she had there. "It doesn't seem sudden to me. I've been steadily falling for you since the moment I met you."

She gulped, realizing with certainty that he meant it. She wasn't alone on this unexpected tightrope of feelings. She visibly sagged with relief, the fight leaving her. "But I barely know you. I ... I don't even know how you take your coffee," she ended lamely.

He chuckled. "We haven't been assigned a profile piece on each other you know. We can discover colorful anecdotes, and likes and dislikes along the way."

He had a point. What was the rush? "You're right," she conceded. "Discovery is the fun part, right?"

"Not the only fun part." He smiled devilishly, capturing her chin with his hand. "But to answer your question about how I prefer my coffee— hot and sweet, just like you." With that, he bent in for another quick but firm and reassuring kiss. Intertwining their hands, he said, "Come on, our pumpkin awaits, and Natalie will have our asses if we ruin her time line."

"I can feel her eye daggers on me already," Eve added, enjoying that her playful comment caused his smile to deepen. She puffed with pride at the simple accomplishment.

"How do *you* like yours?" Adam murmured as they headed toward the idling bus.

"Huh?"

"Your coffee."

"Oh. Dark and strong, just like you."

He beamed. Adam had made his feelings clear and she could not deny hers. This was more than attraction. Emotions were winning over logic. She wanted everything he was offering and damned the consequences.

Screw PDA and professionalism, she leaned up on the tips of her sandy toes and returned his kiss, briefly flicking her tongue out to taste his lower lip. Both his curse and the hunger electrifying his dark eyes said he was fighting back the urge to deepen their embrace. She did too, but not here, not now.

Giggling, she ran toward the group, knowing his eyes were on her.

21

Disembarkation day was a somber event. They were assigned the earliest listed departure time and were jarred back to reality with another early wake-up call. The crew needed everyone out as soon as possible so they could ready the ship for the next round of lucky, incoming passengers.

Time for reality. Today, their normal, extravagant, dining room breakfast was reduced to a quick bite, but that was fine with Adam. After this lavish trip, the last thing he needed was to eat more food. Besides, his stomach was currently tied up in knots regarding his relationship with Eve. Neither of them had been brave enough to discuss next steps.

He for sure didn't want this to be only a vacation fling. None of that "what happens on a cruise stays on a cruise" bullshit. No, he wanted a lot more. More of Eve and no more pretending. While he was certain their connection was real, he wasn't sure how to broach it without botching things. He only wished his circumstances were different. That he had more to offer her. Most of all, he had to figure a few things out first.

They walked down the gangway side by side, stealing unsure glances at one another, both not saying anything. At customs, they were separated and directed to different passport control lines by a no-nonsense TSA agent who was quick to point out that they were not a family unit traveling together. Adam's queue moved much quicker, so he went in search of their luggage, which had been brought on land while they slept. Not that they had really slept much. He grinned, remembering how she'd been the one to wake him up before dawn to make love again. He hadn't needed much encouragement, already missing their intertwined bodies.

Everything in her eyes last night told him she felt every ounce of desire that he did, and it humbled him. He'd wanted her for what felt like a lifetime and now she wanted him in return. Once again, a heady feeling surged though his veins as if he'd just been injected with a drug that was all Eve. He had to stop himself from whistling like a happy fool right there in the baggage claim area.

Adam spotted Eve's loud, tropical-print, hard-shell suitcase right away. Frankly, the neon beacon would have been hard to miss. No doubt another travel tip of hers. His army-issued duffel bag, meanwhile, was wedged behind a trunk and a fallen suitcase. Assessing the situation, he squatted. Lifting from his knees, he dislodged the trapped bag with one swift movement, hefting it up onto his right shoulder with ease.

"Whoa," came a voice from behind that Adam immediately recognized as Hugh's even before he turned to scowl. He was surprised, though, to find the man was shuffling his feet and wouldn't meet his eyes. "Uh ... one second, mate."

Adam patiently waited for Hugh to get his words out, already set on edge by his unexpectedly friendly tone. "Listen, I ... that is to say, *Hugh*, better take care of her," Hugh finally said with a sad smile.

Adam almost lost his grip on his duffel. He wasn't sure what to say or what angle the guy was playing at. Perhaps, in his own jealous haze, he'd judged Hugh too strongly.

"I know I buggered things up with Eve," Hugh continued with a prolonged sigh. "I should have put her first, but I just don't think it's in me. I hope you're able to do a better job because she really is a lovely person and deserves it."

Stunned, Adam simply nodded as Hugh left, rolling his monogram-embroidered, leather bags with swivel wheels. His words lingered, though. Could Adam do a better job? He was in love with Eve, he was sure of it, but he feared loving her would hold her back. He was confined to his tiny world, dammit. He wasn't free to take off whenever the mood struck him. He had responsibilities. Besides, he'd already achieved many of his career goals, and she was just beginning to take on hers. When it came to her career, he probably wasn't any better for her than Hugh. *Shit.*

He didn't mean to clam up on their car ride back to their coast of Florida, but he was too busy working it all out in his head. Surely, he could solve this problem so that it added up to a different answer than the one he kept arriving at.

Eve tried to engage him with her constant, cheery chatter, but he kept his responses short, his thoughts focused on what he should do versus what he wanted to do, which was grovel at her tiny, painted feet and beg her to have him. He clung to his remaining self-control and didn't, of course. Still, he couldn't help but grasp her hand, just so he could touch her, not wanting to let go even though he knew it wasn't right. *He* wasn't right for her. Hell, it took him clearing several obstacles just to make this trip work.

"Who's getting dropped off first?" Eve asked, breaking through his inner turmoil and head trash.

"A gentleman always sees a lady home properly," he replied.

She pursed her lips in frustration, and fuck, he wanted to kiss them. Kissing Eve was heaven, and he longed to do it forever, but kissing her made him yearn for more. And more was what he couldn't give her. Even if his heart and mind desperately wanted to.

When they eventually arrived back at her apartment complex, he carried her bags to the front door. She invited him inside, suggesting she'd drive him home later. Declining took all his willpower. "Another time," he gritted out, needing to get away before he carried her through her entryway and placed her on any solid surface that would do. Then buried his frustration inside her, absorbed her sweetness, and claimed her once again to block out the injustice of it all. Instead, he clenched the screen door until his knuckles turned white.

Her bright smile slid away from her face and her shoulders stiffened. She was hurt by his refusal. Hell, he was hurting, too—big time. He took a deep breath to steady himself and to keep from crossing over the entryway, only to inhale her beckoning, earthy, sweet scent in the process. Forcing a smile he didn't feel, he tried his best to gentle his tone. "Go ahead and unpack. We'll see one another at work tomorrow."

She nodded, her big baby blues pinning him further to the spot. How the hell was he going to walk away from her when he couldn't even step back from her doorway? Leaning up, she placed a hand on his chest and her lips on his unshaven cheek. The resulting ringing in his ears kept him from hearing whatever goodbyes she'd uttered. He briefly pictured breaking down her door like Fred Flintstone, but somehow, he managed to get his wooden legs moving and back to the waiting cab.

22

Eve hated having to say goodbye, even if it was just temporary. Trying not to take it personally, she called a very triumphant Jada who'd somehow managed to say, "I knew it" and "I told you so," only about a dozen times. Thankfully, her friend's enthusiasm was contagious, and Eve was beaming once again, even humming to herself, while she unpacked like the lovesick fool that she was.

They'd spent seven straight days together. It was probably best that Adam hadn't stayed over tonight, too. A little space was a good thing, and she was just being overly sensitive about his refusal to enter her small but comfy abode.

Sure, she had a travel magazine pile that threatened to be taller than her soon, and several boxes still yet to be unpacked. Otherwise, she kept her place clean, almost sparse. Most of her sentimental belongings and knickknacks were stored up in Ohio at her family home. After her breakup, she wasn't sure how long she'd stay in Southwest Florida, but she'd since made friends and headway with her career, and now there was Adam, too. She wasn't traveling as often, either. Maybe she could get a pet. Either way, it was time to start making her home more ... lived in. She'd begin by filling the hand-painted, ceramic, mosaic-tile picture frame she'd purchased in Mexico, which she'd placed on her nightstand before getting under the covers.

An hour later, she was still awake, tossing and turning in bed. What would it be like at work tomorrow? She pictured silly scenarios of stilted greetings, all the while playing footsies under the table. Or sneaking a quick embrace in the kitchen. No, that would be too risky and unprofessional. Still, that led to some other dirty, work fantasies that had her tossing and turning in sexual frustration instead.

But Monday, Eve arrived at work only to find Adam's desk was still empty. When he finally did show up, it was just a moment before their morning meeting started. He gave her a brisk nod and took a seat across the conference table despite the open chair right next to her, which Carl then took before peppering her with a dozen questions about her trip. She did her best to answer and not give in to her desire to look over at Adam, whose mere presence had her body snapping to attention. It took most of her concentration to ignore the pull.

"Carl, do you mind?" Nik asked, as he stood in front of the calendar. Poor Carl blushed, which only aided in reminding everyone of how junior he was. She gave him a sympathetic smile and a pat on his arm while Nik officially started the meeting.

"I read through your submission, Adam, and well done," Nik said to the entire group. "It was funny, actually, something I never thought I'd say about your writing."

Adam chuckled. "Thank you, I guess."

Eve couldn't help but smile with pride and delight. Also, a little jealous that Nik had the opportunity to read his piece first. It wasn't even due to the editorial desk until tomorrow, and Eve was still finishing up her portion.

"I sent it to the fact-checkers to confirm details with the cruise line, but we should be good to go for Thursday's travel edition with plenty of time for our sister pubs to include in their Sunday magazines."

"That's great," Eve voiced in, continuing to smile. "You'll have my version by end of day."

Nik nodded. "I'd like for this to be a regular travel feature, highlighting other destinations. Bi-monthly maybe."

Eve was ready to bounce up and down in her seat, but Adam's stern reply stilled her. "That's not possible."

"Fine, monthly," Nik said dismissively, clicking over to the next name on the displayed list.

"I can't," Adam gritted out, and Eve sat up straighter, almost pitching her rocking seat forward. She tried to catch Adam's gaze and give him a "what's going on" look, but his dark glare was targeted on Nik alone.

"Not this again," Nik said, massaging his temples.

"That's great about an ongoing feature," Adam said smoothly, "but I don't need to be involved. Eve is quite capable of doing it solo."

"Of course, she is." Nik puffed his chest out, shooting her a nervous look and shifting back and forth on his feet. "You are," he restated, and she nodded back. What else could she do?

"Excursions with Eve," Adam suggested.

"Oh, good alliteration," Carl chimed in with his usual enthusiasm.

"Carl, would you rather work in advertising? They have an opening," Nik snapped, and Carl slouched in his seat. The kid made himself too easy of a target.

"Excursions with Eve" did have a nice ring to it, but she continued to stare at Adam, trying her best to decipher what he wasn't saying. What would be so bad about an occasional tag team and trip?

Nik swiveled his head between her and the adamant Adam Seager. *Maybe that's where his name came from,* she thought, irked. Instead of footsies as she'd previously imagined, she would much rather kick him under the table right now. Hard.

"It's the gimmick of the two voices that is intriguing and what the other competitors are lacking," Nik qualified.

"Let's talk about this offline," Adam said, glancing at his Swiss Army watch with a quick flick of his wrist. "I have to leave now for the city council meeting."

Nik groaned and turned to his assistant. "Inez, when do I have an opening?"

"You have availability at five this evening," Inez chimed in.

"Fine," Adam clipped out, grabbing his satchel and exiting through the glass doors, leaving Eve staring in his wake.

Fine? She sure wasn't fine. She wanted to hurl her Cattyshack Cat Café coffee mug at him, and she loved that local spot and the memento they gave her after she'd covered their grand opening. Why was he doing this? Yes, she appreciated his championing of her writing ability, but she didn't understand his continued refusal of them being writing partners.

If she wasn't feeling so miserable, she might have laughed at the irony that her ex was begging to work with her and her current whatever refused to. Sure, lifestyle and travel weren't his expertise, but he'd seemed to be enjoying it. Not to mention, it would provide them with the chance to travel once a month together like the blissful few days they'd just experienced. Unless, he didn't want that?

She shook her head, doing her best to clear her own negativity. She refused to think the worst. She'd been wrong before about men, but not this time. She was sure of it. Wasn't she? He'd explain his reasons to her, and maybe he'd even change his mind. She shrugged, and if he didn't, that was fine, too, so long as she was still assigned larger-reaching travel pieces like these. She wanted to be on her own when it came to writing anyway. Still, the ambiguity had her nerves jittering like she was on her second cup of coffee instead of halfway through her first.

Eve's mood continued to sink as the day dragged on without so much as a glance of Adam. At noon, she tried peeking her head into Jada's office, but she was on a conference call and gave her a sorry shake of her head, indicating she was too busy to stop for lunch. With no other choice, Eve tried to bury herself in her piece, even though writing about their trip brought back every memory they'd shared together. It was a colorful feature, though. She could feel the words spilling from her fingertips with ease. She even laughed aloud while recounting their cliff-jumping experience, and her stomach grumbled as she described the exotic delights they'd feasted on.

The moment Adam arrived back at work, she could sense it as sure as if someone had turned on a light switch, an invisible force tuning her into his wavelength. But he didn't so much as look her way. Instead, he stalked toward Nik's office, strode through the open door, and shut it behind him with enough strength that it bounced back open, not clicking tight.

Eve debated a few minutes on whether she should join them. She *did* have a stake in the game, after all. Besides, if

Adam was intent on speaking about the future of their column, shouldn't she be there to participate? Riled, she took a deep breath and strode across the room to the slightly ajar door.

"Any other employee here would be jumping at the chance at the occasional free trip. It would just be a week here and there. What's the big deal?" Nik asked, glaring at him but not bothering to get up from behind his cluttered desk.

"The big deal?" Adam echoed. "You know I can't just take off like that. Do you know all the mountains I had to move to make this last trip work?" He didn't bother hiding his exasperation. Staying away from Eve today had drained him, but he needed this whole column thing settled first, and his so-called friend wasn't having his back.

"Is this about Tracy?" Nik asked, his tone gentling vaguely.

"Of course it's about her. You know damn well she's the reason why I moved down here in the first place. The reason why I'm even working here." Frustrated, Adam wanted to throw something, preferably one of Nik's stupid Star Trek bobbleheads he claimed were collector's items.

"Gee thanks, bro," Nik said. "I thought it was the chance to work with me again."

Adam arched a pointed eyebrow at Nik.

"Okay, so I used to report to you, but this is a different beast than *The Washington Post*. Believe me, I'm doing you a favor. You would hate the politics of being the editorial director here and dealing with advertising."

"I don't want your job, Nik, or a new one with Eve. Hell, I don't know what I freakin' want anymore. It's been too long since I even had a say in the matter."

"Well, there you go. Isn't it about time?" Nik asked, pushing up on the leather armchair cushions to finally rise from his seat and step forward.

Adam shrugged. Nik was right, but easier said than done. In a rare, awkward embrace, Nik clamped a hand on his shoulder.

"Are you still living there?" Nik asked.

Adam nodded, glancing toward the door. He shut it with a swift jab of his elbow until he heard the click. "I know, it's time, and things have been getting progressively worse," he said, more to himself than to his friend. He kept telling himself it was the right move, but it still felt like he was abandoning her just the same. "I'm looking at other places nearby."

Nik turned back to his desk, searching for something. He threw a few papers carelessly to the floor before locating an open container filled with unorganized business cards. He pulled it forward and shifted through the contents. "Ah, here you go," he said, shoving a card at Adam with a woman's face on it. "Serina Spring, the best new realtor in town. Carl did a profile on her last month, and I've met her at a few chamber events. She's also engaged to an investor buddy of mine. She is a former city mouse, like you, and hungry. She'll find you something great in no time."

The lack of a realtor wasn't the reason Adam had been dragging his feet, but he slipped the card in his pocket anyway and thanked his friend.

Nik returned his hand to Adam's shoulder to stop him from leaving. "We'll put the 'Adam and Eve Says' column on the back burner for now, but I'm telling you, I know it's going to be a big win for us and for you. Once you get things settled, maybe we can figure out something that works better with your schedule and responsibilities," Nik said, sounding more like his friend and not the editorial director. "And let me know how I can help. I'd be happy to check in on Tracy for you, too."

He doubted that would help but appreciated his friend's belated offer. "Thank you, I'll keep you posted." Once he knew more himself.

Leaving Nik's office, Adam immediately headed to find Eve. He needed to explain himself, but her desk was empty, and her laptop and purse were gone, too. His heart plummeted into his stomach, and he had to wipe his wet palms on his pants. He would fix this. He had to.

23

Tracy? Who the hell was Tracy?

Eve hadn't meant to eavesdrop. She'd had every intention of knocking on the slightly open door to join the debate, but their conversation had stopped her mid-action. Instead, she stood there, frozen, with her fist afloat like she was the newsroom's personal Statue of Liberty.

Tracy was the reason he'd moved to Naples? She'd just solved the big mystery of why he was working here, and it was because of some woman. *She* was the reason he'd given up life in the reporting fast lane. And apparently, he still lived with her.

Eve shuffled out into the parking lot like a zombie. The tears that threatened to fall were blurring her peripheral vision.

"Whoa, Eve, are you okay?" Jada called out to her from one of the rarely used plastic patio tables in front of the building, especially not during a Florida summer. Eve swiveled her head to seek out her voice. Jada was on a call again, but she had her palm over the mouthpiece.

"He lives with Tracy," Eve supplied. Someone he cared

so much about that he moved here for her, gave up his career for her, and never even mentioned it.

"Huh?" Jada asked, before remembering she had someone waiting on the line. She muttered, "Hold on" to whoever it was.

"It's okay," Eve said, waving off her friend's advance. "I'll tell you later. I have to go." She ran to her car. She couldn't talk about it here, or she'd break down right in front of their place of work. This was why you didn't mix work with pleasure. She knew better, dammit.

She tried to reason with herself as she drove home, but the pep talk wasn't helping settle the ache in her stomach, eating at her as if she'd swallowed Pac Man.

Maybe Tracy was his daughter? If so, why the big secret? Whoever she was, though, he hadn't trusted her enough to clue her in.

Letting herself into her apartment, Eve kicked off her shoes and let the tile floor cool her aching feet before plopping down on her couch, not motivated to do much else. How could she feel so raw and beat up when they were only together for a few days? *It was a fun vacation, be happy with that.* The gnawing ache inside her clearly disagreed with her logic. How could she be so weak as to be rendered a teary mess over what was likely just a little crush. *Then why do I feel so empty inside? Because it felt like more!* The possibilities for them had seemed endless and magical. Adam had made her believe there was magic in love again. The revelation gave her pause.

And why was she upset? Because he had a past? She'd had a fiancé before, after all. But Adam had known about Hugh. She had nothing to hide, but what did she know about Tracy? Or Adam, for that matter, outside of being an amazing lover and writer.

No, he'd shown her a different side of him on their trip. He'd been raised by a single mother, lost his father at age fourteen, liked to gamble, twitched and mumbled in his sleep with what she feared could be classified as PTSD nightmares. He was also a jaw-dropping diver, an astounding dancer, and incredibly witty. He was the reason she smiled a thousand smiles. She needed him for all those things and so many other intangible reasons. Most of all, she'd loved how he made her feel—spe-cial, wanted. Yup, she was screwed. Not to mention, he genuinely wanted her to succeed.

Her cell phone chirped with an incoming text message. About time Jada checked on her after fleeing like she had. Although, Eve wasn't up for dinner with her friend and her adorable family. The mere thought made her feel more miserable. Sighing, she picked up the phone, already forming an excuse in her head, but the message wasn't from Jada. The notification indicated that it was from "Adam Work."

Hey you. Sorry for the busy day. Are you free to meet in an hour to talk?

Just like that? He expected her to run because he finally wanted to talk? Unsure of her answer, her thumbs hovered over the digital keypad before she replied, short and sweet.

Why don't you talk to Tracy?

The bubbles in the chat window showed he'd already been typing something, but her reply must have stopped him as they disappeared again. *Good.* She hoped she'd shocked him like he'd done to her.

Please? I can explain.

Then do it, she mumbled aloud. Before she could respond, his subsequent text chirped into view.

Come on, you owe me.

That did it! She needed to get this owing him business cleared up once and for all. Despite her anger, the idea of paying that debt with her body flitted through her mind just the same. Besides, the reporter in her knew she was missing some of the key facts to his story and wanted to hear his explanation. She just had to keep her emotions in check until she learned more.

Fine. Where?

My place? In an hour? I'll send you a pin drop.

So, she was going to finally know where the elusive Adam Seager lived. She tapped a thumbs-up sign and stood to change. Even if they were about to break up, her pride demanded she look her very best.

24

Forty-five minutes later, despite following the turn-by-turn instructions on her phone's GPS, Eve ended up in a parking lot behind a retirement building where an idle ambulance waited. Parking in an empty space, she grabbed her phone to inspect the map and the original pin Adam had sent and replied to their conversation.

I think you sent me the wrong address. This is an assisted living and memory care center.

He texted back.

You're in the right spot. I'll be right out.

She turned off her car and stepped outside, taking in the peaceful grounds as she waited. It was so posh and serene, if not for the sign out front, she'd have thought it was a country club or golf community. Adam strode out of the lobby entrance in the distance. Just seeing him sent a punch to her gut. He nodded to a woman in scrubs who was pushing an elderly man in a wheelchair.

Eve sat down lightly on the hood of her car and waited for Adam to reach her. His face looked weary, his steps less confident than usual. Still, when his dark eyes locked on hers, the air rushed from her lips.

"I thought we were going to meet at your home?" she asked the moment he'd neared, not bothering with a proper greeting.

He shoved his hands in the pockets of his cargo slacks, looking boyish. "This is my home."

"Excuse me?"

He nodded. "I live here with my mother, *Tracy*. She's seventy-four and has stage-five dementia in severe cognitive decline."

His mother? She hadn't seen that coming. "I ... I'm sorry to hear that," she said, reeling.

He shrugged his shoulders and leaned on the hood alongside her, their hands brushing, sending the usual sizzle of electricity through her. They sat there in silence for a moment. His gaze focused on the memory care home in front of them while Eve stared at his profile, waiting for him to continue.

"I tried taking care of her on my own, I really did, but it got to the point I couldn't even leave the house without an incident. She'd forget to turn off the stove or roam outside and not remember how to get back. Her doctor eventually recommended Sunny Pines, which is why I moved down here, but it's also expensive as hell. Now, at least, she's getting constant care and sometimes recognizes me at the end of the day."

She bit her lip and leaned closer to him. A tropical breeze swept his dark hair. She wanted to smooth it back, hug him, do anything to relieve his pain and provide comfort. But she wanted to hear the whole story first. "So, you live here, too?"

"Yeah," he said, crossing his arms. "They typically only

allow spouses in the assisted living housing, but they made an exception, and in the beginning, they even said my presence was helping."

"Not anymore?"

"No," he said on an exhale, shoving a hand through his hair. "She still knows who I am for the most part, but she also thinks it's twenty years ago and that I spend the day in school when I'm not with her. Other times, she thinks I'm my father, or worse, a stranger."

Not able to resist, she stroked his arm, feeling his pain wash over her. "That must be very difficult. I know you two are very close. I'm so sorry. But Adam, you're still young. You can't give up your entire life for her."

He pulled back, her hand hovering in the air. "Can't I? When my father died, she still made sure I had the best of everything and took on a weekend retail job. Not to mention how I put her nerves through hell when I was deployed abroad, leaving her during her good years."

"But that's what kids do. You can't put your own life on hold during *your* good years. I don't know Tracy, but no mom would want that for her child."

Her truth stopped whatever he had been about to say. Instead, he closed his mouth and nodded. "The thing is, if I'm away for too long, it takes weeks to get her mind back in the right decade. That's why I can't travel."

Her heart ached, seeing the pain etched across his face and the internal struggle and pressure he must be going through. While she didn't really understand, not being in the same situation, she could see why he felt anchored here. "You could have just told me."

"I know, I intended on doing so," he admitted. "I'm not used to talking about it, and selfishly, I was afraid to blow things with you before they had even started."

That made her smile. "Okay," she said. "I get that."

He gave her one of his teasing smiles back, and it was like a fist wrapping around her heart. "Yeah, like how you don't go around advertising that you snore."

His dig caught her off guard more than the simultaneous, playful nudge his elbow had. "I do not snore," she protested.

"Yeah, you do. It's kinda cute. Although on our bus ride, I had to jostle you a bit so others wouldn't hear such cuteness."

She chuckled, enjoying stepping into their old repartee. It gave her the strength to ask the question she really needed answered. "All right, so I get that we can't be Adam and Eve, the writing team, but we can still be Adam and Eve the couple, right?"

"Honestly, I don't see how it can work," he said, his voice low with emotion.

The air rushed from her lips once again. So that was what a sucker punch to the gut felt like. Not that she had ever wondered or wanted to know. But his words had the same chilling effect. Jumping up, she turned to stand in front of him so she could clearly see his face and read him better. "So, that's it? You just changed your mind? Scratched an itch or something?"

"God, no! Baby, I want to be with you, but I don't want to hold you back. You need to be free and pursue your dreams. I don't want to be another Hugh in your life. You deserve the world, Eve, and I'm stuck here."

"But ... but can't I have the world with you?" she asked, hearing the desperation in her voice and refusing to shy away from it. Damn her pride—Adam was worth fighting for, even if she had to beg or kick some sense into him so that he understood that.

"Besides there are worse places to be stuck than Southwest Florida."

He shook his head. "Traveling is your passion, and your work. You have your whole career ahead of you. Believe me, I'd love to be by your side, but right now, I can't give you one hundred percent, and it's killing me. I want to be your writing partner, to take off with you and continue our column, or simply be there to hold your notepad, whatever."

"It doesn't have to be all or nothing, Adam. I want to be by your side, too, and that includes your challenges. Let's figure this out together." She reached for him, slipping her hands into his and squeezing, forcing his dark gaze back up to hers.

"You don't understand," he said, groaning, and pulling her closer, despite his stricken words. "I can't even take you back home to my place. I can barely get away at night, and you deserve all that and so much more."

The more he protested, the more she knew she was right about him. He was only trying to protect her and take care of his family, and she refused to let him keep them apart for such noble reasons. Taking a deep breath she clamped down her frustration with his stubborness. Stepping between his legs, she leaned down to brush her lips against his.

She smiled inwardly when he tried to deepen the caress, but she tilted her head back, leaving his puckered lips hovering in the air between them. That was all she needed to know. He *did* want her, no matter what he said about why they couldn't be something more.

"Stop focusing on *can't*," she insisted. "You can challenge me, you can inspire me, you can make my body tremble, you can—"

"I can love you," he butted in, his voice cracking slightly.

"I already do. I love you, Eve. You're every dream I've ever had come to life, plus qualities I wanted and didn't even know existed until I discovered them in you." Her heart expanded in her chest, bumping against her ribs. "But it's not about me," he continued. "I want the best for you, that's all. No regrets, no holding you back."

"Good, because my only regret would be letting you go," she declared, flinging herself into his arms and loving how he wrapped them around her, smashing her tight against his solid frame, curling her face into his warm neck. She placed a kiss in the hollow at the base of his throat, sucking at the tender flesh and wanting more.

He drew her away and regarded her with a frown. "Are you sure, love?"

Her heart filled with love just hearing him say the words again. Lifting her mouth back to meet his, she let her kiss give him the answer. But before she got overly distracted, and while she still had a thought in her head, she remembered what she'd been about to say and lifted her face to look up at his. "You were right before when you said you're not Hugh. Your concern for my career only proves it and none of these obstacles are dealbreakers. I'm sure Nik will eventually concede to letting me continue the feature solo or assign another male POV if it's really needed."

"Well, then, I just hope on future trips you insist on your own room," he deadpanned, and she laughed, relief filling her lungs.

"Obviously! Besides, you're missing the most important fact, Seager."

"What's that?" he asked, no absurd endearments to his question, genuine concern in his voice.

"I love you, too," she declared proudly.

He stared deeply into her eyes, as though questioning

her sincerity, and she nodded in emphasis, compelled with the urge to grab his skeptical face in a reassuring kiss. His smile was slow at first but ended huge. "Thank you," he said, laying reverent kisses all over her face to the point that she couldn't help but laugh at his exuberance and from sheer happiness.

"Plus, you, of all people, should know that the beauty of writing is that I can work from anywhere. Even if I one day pen my own guide, I'd only have to travel for a few weeks at a time, but then there are weeks of compiling my notes, writing, and rewriting. I can do that wherever you are. If you want me, that is."

"Fuck yes, I want you, in every way possible."

He kissed her again, before pulling back to speak once more. "I ... uh ... actually have an appointment with a realtor to see a condo a few miles away from Sunny Pines. It's a two bedroom with an extra loft area that could double as an office with a balcony overlooking one of those fake lakes. I've only seen the pictures on my phone, but I swear I imagined you writing there. I know it's way too early, but ... *you* feel like home to me and I haven't had a home in a really long time. I guess what I'm royally messing up, but trying to say is that I'm finally ready to start living my life again—with you. Because of you. Does any of that make sense?"

She nodded and blinked back the tears gathering in her eyes, not wanting to ruin this beautiful moment being a crying mess. "Yes, and god, I want that, too." Leaning up on her tippy toes, she kissed him again because she couldn't help herself. "Besides, I owe you, right?"

He froze beneath her lips, and she broke apart to see what was going on. She'd been joking of course.

"You don't owe me anything," he said, sounding serious when she'd only meant to tease.

"I ... I thought you were counting—fake boyfriend, dismissed ticket ..."

"About that ticket," he said, looking down at the ground guiltily. "Since I'm coming clean with everything else, there's something I should tell you. Um ... why do you think O'Malley was even patrolling outside your community that morning?"

She did a double take. "Wait, what? You arranged *that*? Why?"

He gave her a lopsided grin. "I had to break through to you somehow, and frankly, I was getting desperate. After all, I wasn't expecting to have the gift of a working vacation with you dropping into my lap."

"So, you had me pulled over?" she asked, aghast.

"Then swooped in to save the day," he pointed out with a an awkward shrug. "Smooth, no?"

"Like sandpaper," she grumbled, although really, she wanted to preen with pleasure. He'd gone through all those hoops just to get her attention. It was romantic, in a heavy-handed misuse of power sort of way.

Adam shifted in front of her with what looked like anxious uncertainty. "Come on, smooches, no harm, no foul." He reached out to grab her, but she evaded.

"Let me get this straight," she said, placing her hands on her hips and doing her best to stay stern. "Despite your manipulations, you were going to collect on this debt?"

"Hell, yes. I never lied about my intent there," he said, laughing. "But I was just hoping we'd go out to happy hour, or dinner, as a means to pay me back, and then, of course, I'd unload all my charms on you and pray for a real date."

It would have worked. His charms were a force to be reckoned with. "Hmm ... I think you owe *me* now for tricking me."

He beamed. "Anything," he said, playfully smacking her on the ass. "Just name your price, Richards."

She paused for a moment, thinking of a dozen pleasing scenarios before settling on an important one. "Can I meet your mom, when you're ready, that is?"

He visibly swallowed. "I'd love that, but I can't promise what frame of mind she'll be in. Although, if she were to see you regularly with me, she might keep the connection. It's been the case with some of the caregivers here. I know she'd like the company, either way."

"Me too. Plus, I'd like to thank her for dragging you to dance lessons and for raising such an amazing guy."

"Damn, can you be any more perfect?"

She shook her head. "I'm not perfect, but you definitely make me wish I was."

"You're perfect for me," Adam corrected. This time, she willingly went back into his arms when he reached for her and with enough force that they fell back on her car hood. Laughing, he righted them once more, still keeping her circled in his arms.

"What, no more silly nicknames?" she asked, hugging him tight and deeply breathing him in.

"I thought you hated them," he said into her hair as he nuzzled her closer.

"Not all of them," she said, scoffing.

"Sugar lips?" he asked, bending his head to snack on them.

"Definitely not that one," she managed to mutter into his mouth.

"It's true, though. Your lips do taste like sugar, and I'm addicted to them." He kissed her deeper, emphasizing his point, tangling his hand in her hair as he tilted her head to bring the kiss to a carnivorous level.

She kissed him back with all the love and pleasure she felt being there with him. If only they weren't outside in a parking lot, or she'd surely tackle him to the ground and really demonstrate how much.

As if reading her mind, he looked over his shoulder before resting their foreheads together. His dark-brown eyes penetrated hers, sending chills throughout her body, despite the heat outside.

"How about, my love?" he asked earnestly.

"Now, that's perfect."

Just like their life would be. She knew it. There would be challenges, of course, she wasn't naïve. But they'd have each other, and man, did that feel empowering. "You're 'my love,' too," she whispered against the hollow beneath his jaw.

She sighed with contentment. This was better than any story she'd covered and after all her travels, she felt at home too just being here in his arms.

......

ALSO BY TARA SEPTEMBER

Mine to Five

Jesse's Girl

It Might Be You (Short Story)

MINE TO FIVE
'TIS THE SEASON FOR AN OFFICE ROMANCE

CHAPTER ONE

Nothing good can come from another woman answering your guy's cell phone.

Melanie Thomas came to this epiphany the moment she heard the unfamiliar female voice on the other end of the phone line. She did a double take to make sure she'd selected the correct name from her contact list, but sure enough, clear as day, it read Joe. *Her* Joe.

He didn't have a sister either and his mother had passed away. That left three likely possibilities. None were pleasant, and all spelled doom for her relationship.

Possibility number one, would go something like, "Hello this is Mrs. Kinnear, please stop calling my husband, you tramp!"

Melanie dismissed the idea as quickly as it surfaced. After almost two years of dating, surely she would have ferreted out a wife by now, right?

Possibility number two, the mystery woman was a concerned police officer, medic or bystander who would solemnly say, "I am so sorry to be the one to inform you, but there has been a terrible accident. His last request is to see your beautiful face again. Please hurry!"

She really shouldn't hope for this scenario, but a horrible, selfish part of her preferred it to the last option.

No, sadly, possibility number three was the most probable reason for why another woman was answering her boyfriend's phone at night. Even her shocked mind registered this option was more like probability number one. Her boyfriend was having an affair, plain and simple, or rather pain and simple.

"Hello?" the feminine voice repeated after Melanie had failed to get her tongue-tied mouth to answer the first time.

From her voice alone Melanie could tell the other woman had to be sexy. Her predatory purr dripped of confidence laced with a tinge of malice.

Melanie cringed, but she managed to ask over the peach-sized pit lodged in her throat, "Is Joe Kinnear there?" Sucking in her breath, she braced for the unknown woman's answer.

"Of course, let me wake him up," taunted the sultry, young voice.

Wake him up? She hunched forward from the invisible sucker punch. *Yup, definitely scenario three. He's cheating!*

Staring at the blue glow from her phone, she noticed the call time count. Twenty seconds, that was how long it took to unravel a relationship of twenty months. Cradling the phone in the crook of her neck, Melanie covered her other ear with her palm and tried to block out the noise of the busy club as she waited.

To think, moments earlier she had been eager for the night ahead, especially since Joe had something important to discuss with her. That, paired with the fact that she was celebrating the start of a new job at a major advertising firm tomorrow—a job that would make her career—had Melanie elated as she'd walked through the steel doors of the trendy Manhattan nightclub Surge. Everything in her life had seemed to be aligning for her. The tide had finally been turning, and Melanie was more than ready to have it roll her way. It had all been going as planned, except now it wasn't.

∼

Now Available!

ABOUT THE AUTHOR

Blogger and former PR executive, Tara holds a Master's degree in journalism and communications from New York University. For over a decade, she has penned a popular lifestyle, travel and parenting blog at TaraMetBlog.com.

An avid romance reader, she has been daydreaming about being a romance author since high school. Dozens of bad dates and adventures later, she still finds it impossible that she met her husband on a New York City subway. Now they live in sunny Southwest Florida with identical twin boys, and four cats underfoot. When the kids are asleep and the cats are not lying on her keyboard, she's finally writing the happily ever after tales she's been dreaming about. www.TaraSeptember.com

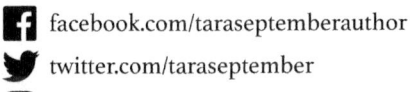

- facebook.com/taraseptemberauthor
- twitter.com/taraseptember
- instagram.com/taraseptemberauthor

Printed in Great Britain
by Amazon